KNIGHT OF THE CROSS

A Knight Hospitaller novella

by Steven A. McKay

Copyright 2014 Steven A. McKay

Also by Steven A. McKay:

Wolf's Head

The Wolf and the Raven

"There are horrors beyond life's edge that we do not suspect,

and once in a while man's evil prying calls them just within our range."

H.P. Lovecraft – The Thing on the Doorstep

Rhodes, 1309 AD

The little Greek Orthodox priest was sweating profusely, his black beard almost dripping with moisture, but the wide-eyed look he wore suggested something more than the heat inside the fortress was causing his discomfort.

"What are we to do, Father Vitus?" Foulques de Villaret, Grand Master of the Knights Hospitaller, also known as the Knights of Rhodes, demanded. "We've only just taken full control of the island; my men are needed to maintain law and order and to make necessary repairs to the city. I'd rather not have to send them chasing after some local legend your people haven't been able to get to the bottom of."

For three years de Villaret had overseen the invasion of Rhodes, understanding the strategic importance of its position to his Order. The Hospitallers had previously been based in neighbouring Cyprus but relations with the Cypriot king had been tense and Rhodes offered the ideal position to control the trade routes from the Black Sea. After an impressive land-sea military operation, the Order had finally taken control of the island and was now working to improve the old Byzantine fortifications.

In the past fortnight though, two of the Hospitaller sergeants-at-arms had mysteriously disappeared followed just a couple of days later by an actual knight. All three men had gone missing while visiting Father Vitus's village of Sgourou, which was why the priest had been summoned to the Grand Master's palace.

"I know no more than you," the little Greek clergyman replied. "The people of my village are frightened and angry too. For months these disappearances have gone on, and no-one has ever done anything to help us. My people need action, they need an end to this...abomination! You're wasting your time calling me here; me and my congregation have nothing to do with your soldiers going missing. Whatever is taking these people comes from far outside the city walls, far from my village."

Sir Richard-at-Lee, an Englishman, stood behind his superior with three other high-ranking members of the Order, frowning, not quite sure what to make of Vitus's words. It was hard to follow, in truth: the man could speak French – being, along with Latin the language spoken by the new ruling class on the island – fairly well, but some of the words he was using didn't seem to translate very well and, as a result, it sounded as if he was blaming some kind of ancient demon for the unexplained vanishings in the city.

The Hospitallers were devoted to Christ – they understood the truth of the bible and knew that there were evil forces at work all throughout the world but...Father Vitus's tale seemed too incredible to be true. Surely it was nothing more than the ravings of a few superstitious, uneducated villagers Sir Richard thought.

"What exactly are you saying is causing these disappearances?" The big knight asked, making sure

2

to keep his tone neutral for fear of offending the influential clergyman. The peace on the island was a fragile one at present, as the knights sought to stamp their authority on the place and the people.

The priest shrugged and muttered something in a language none of the Hospitallers present could identify before looking up to meet Sir Richard's eyes. "It is old. Older than the world itself. Some say it came from another place, somewhere far away; maybe even amongst the stars, if such a thing is possible. Whatever it is, I can't say, for I've never seen it and anyone who has is sent insane." He waved a hand at the high-vaulted ceiling vaguely. "But these are just stories to frighten children, or entertain drinkers in a tavern."

"I've heard some of these stories," the Grand Master nodded, gazing at Father Vitus. "Who are the people with the black eyes?"

The priest looked away and Sir Richard watched him closely as he replied. "I've never seen anyone with black eyes; that's just another story. You should forget such nonsense and search the countryside to find the people that took your men. Perhaps they have black eyes out there, at the opposite end of the island."

Foulques de Villaret shook his head. "No. My men went missing when they were visiting your village, so that's where we'll begin our search."

"We don't need your knights, my people will –"

"Silence!" de Villaret rose from his chair and glared down at the priest. The Grand Master was an impressive man, with immaculate hair and a neatly trimmed beard, and his eyes blazed now as his patience ran out. "Your people have, by your own admission, had months to do something about this and haven't managed it. Well, this is *my* island now, and I won't have my men being kidnapped!"

Father Vitus glared back at the knight but held his tongue, knowing he couldn't win this confrontation.

"I can't spare many of my men though. Sir Richard here" – de Villaret waved the English knight forward to stand by his side – "can speak some Greek. He'll take his sergeant-at-arms and follow you to your village where he'll investigate the disappearances. If he finds reason to believe any of this legend is factual, or that you and your people have anything to do with it, then we'll look at sending a more sizeable force into the area to... take care of the problem. Once and for all."

Vitus shook his head at the implied threat. "Very well, but I fear your knight" – he looked Sir Richard up and down – "even one as dangerous-looking as this, won't be enough to solve this mystery." He bowed to the Grand Master, holding onto his black kamilavka so it didn't fall off and gestured to the big Englishman to follow him. "Come, Sir Richard, I'll await you and your sergeant by the main door where the shadows are long and the heat isn't as intense. I suggest you don't wear full armour, or any of your insignia – you may not want to attract attention to yourself when travelling in such a small party, given what happened to your brothers."

Sir Richard knelt to his superior and crossed himself reverentially. "I'll do my best to get to the bottom of this, Grand Master," he said, turning to

4

address Vitus as he strode past him out of the room. "Go to your shadows, father – I'll gather my weapons and my sergeant and meet you shortly. But I'm a Knight of Rhodes and I'll not hide this cross I bear. If anyone has a problem with it, trust me – they'll have more to worry about than some ancient bloody demon!"

* * *

From the citadel to Father Vitus's village of Sgourou was a fair walk of about an hour; along the bustling streets of the city, out through St Anthony's Gate and into the countryside. Sir Richard, followed by his stocky sergeant-at-arms, Jacob, found himself wishing they'd taken horses from the stables for the journey. The priest had walked to the city though, so it seemed rude to ride when he was on foot. Eventually though, Father Vitus told them they were almost there and the knight heaved a sigh of relief.

"We'll pass through the local market," the priest said, biting into a small oatcake he carried as they walked. "If you're observant, maybe you'll see one of the black-eyed people your Grand Master spoke of. Don't meet their gaze if you do," he laughed, "I've heard it's bad luck to do so."

Unconsciously, Sir Richard's hand caressed the pommel of his longsword, irritated by the sniggering Greek priest but wondering how much of this legend was true. Probably none of it, he thought. Yes, he was a devout Christian; that was why he'd joined the

Hospitallers six years ago, despite having a wife and two young sons. He'd been a mercenary – often fighting alongside the Hospitallers or Templars before his martial prowess and natural leadership had been recognized by one of the Hospitallers and he'd been asked to join the Order which accepted married men as long as their spouses agreed. He knew angels and demons existed. The bible said so, didn't it? But black-eyed men that worshipped some ancient evil from a far-off place in the stars...Sir Richard couldn't take it seriously; the whole tale was just too outlandish.

Jacob was too hot and tired to care much, but he met the big knight's gaze, his expression one of nervous uncertainty. Father Vitus had, for the sergeant's benefit, reiterated the tale he'd told to the Grand Master earlier, going into more detail this time as the two Hospitallers questioned him on certain points. The sergeant was naturally more superstitious and inclined to believe in the physical manifestation of devils and ghouls than his sceptical master.

As they came into Sgourou the streets, filled with people going about their daily business at this time in the afternoon, became even busier; the sounds and multitude of smells clamouring upon their senses as they approached the market.

Sellers loudly hawked their wares, from foods like bread and freshly caught fish, to clothing and pottery. Prostitutes eyed the two Hospitallers as they moved through the crowd, but Sir Richard's bearing and stern gaze kept them from approaching. Being outside the city, the stalls held next to nothing of great value; no exotic spices or finely made weaponry here. There was drink, though, and plenty of it.

"Is that cool?" Jacob demanded in English, licking his parched lips at the sight of a collection of tall amphorae containing wine under a thick canopy that kept off the worst of the sun.

"It is, my lord," the seller replied. "Cool, and made from top quality moschato grapes. Try some!" He poured a little from a smaller jug into three wooden cups and handed them to the perspiring men who gratefully knocked them back, sighing in pleasure as the liquid coated their dry throats and filled their bellies with a hint of fire.

"Another three cups, please," Sir Richard asked, in Greek this time, handing the seller a small silver coin, marvelling at the ability of salesmen all around the world to learn just enough of different languages to be able to sell their wares to foreigners from all over. "Water them this time though, we need clear heads."

As the wine-seller poured more of the drink the knight decided they might as well start their investigation immediately. "What do you know of the disappearances around here?" he asked, watching the man's reaction intently.

"Something evil has been taking our people – men, women, boys, girls, it makes no difference. Where they go, who knows? I don't, and I'm glad, for it would send me mad!" The man finished pouring their wine and moved off to serve another thirsty customer, throwing them a final glance over his shoulder as he went. "Wherever they're going it's a bad place. We hear the screaming at night, often. Coming from *under the ground...*"

Sir Richard grunted dismissively, but Jacob shivered, in spite of the heat, as if someone had walked across his grave at the man's words.

"Underground?" The sergeant-at-arms looked down at the dusty street as if it would offer up some clue.

"Nonsense," Father Vitus spat. "There's nothing under these streets but sand."

"It's true," the wine-seller shouted back. "I've heard the noises in the dead of night – we all have. Screams, tortured wails, terrible thumping sounds that seem to come from the very centre of the world." The fear in his eyes was unmistakeable and the two Hospitallers replaced their empty wine-cups onto the seller's table and fell into step behind Father Vitus who walked off towards his church, casting a dark glance at the oblivious merchant.

The wine had been stronger than they'd expected, and the combination of the stifling heat and potent alcohol made Sir Richard and Jacob drowsy. Despite that, both men suddenly turned to stare into the shadows that blanketed the buildings behind them as the uncomfortable sense of being watched came over them.

They could see no one though, so, with a wary glance at each other they followed the Greek priest away from the market towards his parish of St Luke's.

* * *

The Hospitallers were shown to a small room in the

house that adjoined Father Vitus's small church by his housekeeper, a young lady from the distant city of Mosul. She was pretty, and her presence surprised the Hospitallers since she could be a temptation to the clergyman, but she told them that they could sleep there for the duration of their investigation and they nodded their thanks as she backed out of the room, dark eyes fixed on the stone floor.

The soldiers were used to living in austerity, so the simplicity of their temporary room's furnishings meant nothing to them. The atmosphere, however, was another matter.

"Do you feel it?" Jacob muttered, tossing his small pack onto the bed once the housekeeper had left to prepare a frugal meal for the unexpected visitors.

Sir Richard didn't have to ask what his sergeant meant – it was obvious, even to a sceptic like him. The air felt charged with a cloying, suffocating pressure that both depressed and unnerved him. "I do," he admitted. "There's something...unsettling about this place. Not just this room, but the whole village."

"I'm not looking forward to sleeping in here," Jacob agreed, peering out the window. "Ground floor room. Someone could climb in easy enough and slit our throats as we slept! Let's just find out what the hell's going on with these disappearances and get back to the citadel."

Sir Richard grinned, trying to bring some metaphorical light to the oppressive room. "No one'll be able to climb in without waking us," he said. "And I'll be sleeping with my sword in my hand, so anyone who tries will find themselves spitted like a lamb souvlaki!"

They washed their faces in bowls of cool water that had been left in the room for the purpose then made their way to the little dining room where Father Vitus's housekeeper had laid out a light meal for them, consisting of a fresh fish soup and *keftedes,* which were meatballs of pork and herbs in barley flour and fried in olive oil. Neither of the Hospitallers had tasted these dishes before and they enjoyed them very much. Jacob smiled shyly at the housekeeper, thanking her for the meal but she averted her eyes and walked into the kitchen, while Father Vitus glared at the sergeant disapprovingly.

"We're going to go out into the village, "Sir Richard told their host, patting his stomach in satisfaction. "To ask around and see what the villagers can tell us about the disappearances."

The priest nodded assent. "Very well. I don't know how the people will view your presence," he eyed the eight-pointed white cross emblazoned on the Hospitallers' red surcoats, "but perhaps they'll be reassured by the idea that someone's come to put an end to these disappearances that have plagued the area for so long."

"Will you not come with us?" Sir Richard asked, eyeing the man as he licked herbs off his fingers with relish.

"Regretfully, no. I have things to deal with here at the church this evening. You'll be able to find your way around well enough I'm sure – just don't go too far and look for the cross on top of the spire to guide you back home. Here's a key to the front door to save you disturbing Athenais." He looked up almost furtively as the housekeeper came into the room to clear away the dinner dishes. "If I'm not around when you return, please...sleep well."

Meal finished and feeling fully refreshed as the sun had dipped below the horizon, cooling the night air, the soldiers made their way out into the streets which still bustled even at this time. The sounds of laughing and singing filled the air, locals grinned at them, hoisting cups of wine skyward in salute and it seemed like the people were enjoying some celebration.

Sir Richard, a veteran of many battles and a man who'd spent much time in far-flung towns and cities around the world, sensed things weren't quite as they seemed. "Their smiles are forced; tight," he noted, eyes taking in the scenes of apparent revelry around them. "The singing is just a little too loud, as is the laughter. These men and women are frightened, and they use this raucous celebration to mask it – to themselves more than us, I'm sure."

Jacob remained silent, studying the faces around them.

"There," he hissed, nodding surreptitiously to a man just not far in front of them. "Look at his face."

Sir Richard followed his sergeant's stare, the hairs on the back of his neck rising as he saw the swarthy fellow's eyes, the pupils of which were so dilated as to appear almost completely black. As he took in the man's sinister features, the dark eyes suddenly turned and met Sir Richard's.

"Move!" The Hospitaller suddenly roared, tearing full-pelt into the throng of partying people, shoving bodies aside as the man darted into the shadows. "Come on Jacob, don't let him get away!"

The pair sprinted through the streets, barging people out of the way, crashing through stalls selling wine and souvlaki, somehow managing to keep their quarry in sight despite the weight of the chain mail they wore under their crimson surcoats. The people and buildings faded and they realised they were leaving the village, and only the crescent moon lit their pursuit of the black-eyed man.

The thrill of the chase that had coursed through the Hospitallers veins eventually gave way to the monotony of the exhausting run and they could almost feel the gloom closing in around them as they entered what appeared to be another small settlement and their target suddenly began to make a strange keening sound that filled the air, clashing dissonantly with the rhythmic pounding of their feet.

Without warning, their quarry stopped dead in his tracks and stood still, his back to them.

It was so unexpected that Sir Richard grabbed Jacob's arm and the two Hospitallers came to a gasping halt, fingers closing around their sword hilts expectantly.

"You there!" the knight shouted, his voice jarring in the eerie silence. Not a single light burned in the windows of any of the houses around them, although the buildings didn't seem to be derelict. "We just want to talk to you!"

Still panting, trying to draw in lungfuls of night air, Sir Richard watched as the man they'd been chasing at full tilt for such a long distance turned and faced them.

"How's...how's the bastard not out of breath?"

Jacob growled in disbelief. "Look at him!"

It was true. The man glared at them from beneath thick black eyebrows, his body stock still, while the Hospitallers – fit men both of them – heaved with the exertion of the run. His fleshy lips were closed, while his pursuer's mouths were open as they tried to regain their breath.

"You made a mistake coming here," the man said. "And now you will die."

Sir Richard shuddered at the voice – soft, yet somehow horribly repugnant – then he cried out as something hit him hard in his left side. He hauled his longsword from its leather sheath as he stumbled, regaining his footing just in time to ward off the blow that came from the shadowy figure that appeared now from his right.

Jacob had been blind-sided by another assailant and fallen hard, hitting his master as he went down, and he lay now, defenceless, on the hard road as his attacker jumped on top of him, raining blows down on his face and body.

In front of him, Sir Richard brought his sword round in a wide arc that flew harmlessly over his own opponent's head as the man ducked, but the knight had expected the evasive movement and rammed his knee into the side of the man's temple, knocking him to the ground where he lay, cursing but too disoriented to stand up again.

"In the name of Christ!" With a cry the Hospitaller swivelled and swung his sword straight down into the side of Jacob's attacker's skull, feeling the shock of the enormous blow jarring his wrists as the blade lodged tightly in the man's head.

Jacob scrambled out from underneath the dying man as his master jerked his sword free and the pair stood, back to back, eyeing the darkness around them fearfully.

The man Sir Richard had knocked down struggled to rise, a hideous bubbling noise coming from his throat as he looked up at the Hospitaller, eyes wide yet hideously black in the moonlight and his lips pulled back in a grimace.

"Die, you bastard abomination!" Jacob had his own blade out of its sheath by now and he rammed it into the man's neck, straight through, the point bursting in a spray of blood and flesh from the other side. He threw his head back and held his arms wide, screaming with fury and blood-lust as Sir Richard stood silently, trying to regain his breath and marshal his thoughts.

No one else appeared and the silence returned, even more oppressive than before. Their original target had disappeared into the darkness, so they hastily searched the two corpses for anything that might be useful but found nothing other than a scrap of parchment with strange symbols and words scrawled in what appeared to be blood: Ο Ντάγκον έρχεται.

"St John only knows what this is all about," Sir Richard growled, shoving the parchment into an inner pocket, underneath his mail, eyes scanning the few buildings in the settlement for danger. "Come on, let's get back to the church before more of those lunatics appear."

Clouds had covered the night sky by now, obscuring both the moon and the stars so it was impossible for the Hospitallers to get their bearings and, since they'd been so intent on their quarry as they ran, they had no clear idea of how to get back to Sgourou. Eventually though, they found the main road and headed back to Father Vitus's church.

It had been an eventful day...

* * *

They were exhausted when they made it back to St Luke's, having stopped on the way only to buy a couple of skins of wine, a loaf of bread and a wheel of cheese at the local market which was still quite busy despite the late hour. Father Vitus was nowhere to be seen but the housekeeper was standing in the hallway when they came in, her eyes fixed on the floor tiles.

"Would you like anything, my lord?" she asked Sir Richard, avoiding Jacob's lingering gaze.

"No, Athenais, we're fine," the knight replied. "Thank you for asking."

The lady, probably no more than twenty years old Sir Richard guessed, nodded her head, her shoulder length black hair bouncing as she did so and, without looking up made her way towards the kitchen. The men watched as she went then retired to their room where they sat on the beds they'd been assigned, chatting as the strong drink eased their tired muscles and somewhat relaxed them.

"I'm exhausted," Jacob sighed, pulling off his boots and mail shirt. He lay down but placed his

15

dagger beside his pillow with a wary glance towards the window. "Too bloody hot to pull the shutters over," he grumbled. "And you heard what that merchant said earlier, about the noises from underground. Maybe we should set a watch" –

Sir Richard waved the suggestion away with a smile. "Don't be ridiculous! We're safe enough in here. I should set a watch on *you,* perhaps – you seem to have taken a shine to that housekeeper. Just remember your vow of chastity!" He grinned as his sergeant flushed red in embarrassment, spluttering a denial. "Get some sleep; in the morning we'll ask Father Vitus about the place where we were attacked then question some of his congregation about what's going on here. Leave a candle burning if it makes you feel better."

Within a short space of time the Hospitallers were snoring gently, as the sounds of the locals revelling slowly died away and only the noise of insects could be heard outside.

Sir Richard awoke, a sense of impending doom flooding through him and he lay still, wondering what had disturbed his sleep. He could hear nothing but the feeling of intense danger grew in him and he made to reach for the sword that lay propped against the bed by his hand.

Panicking, he realised he couldn't move and he tried to cry out, to warn Jacob, but his mouth wouldn't open. Terrified now, he strained to work his vocal chords, to make *some* kind of sound, even a grunt, but his body refused to respond and he lay, pinned to the straw mattress as...something...came into the room.

Jesus Christ Almighty, what the fuck is that?

The figure was incredibly thin and so black that the shadows seemed to shrink back from its blasphemous outline. Its limbs were long, almost like an insect, but it was so tall that it had to stoop as it approached the knight, despite the high ceiling in the bed chamber. As it approached him, he seemed to hear a whispered chant inside his head, although the words were difficult to make out.

The Hospitaller struggled within himself, every fibre of his soul rebelling against the fear that stopped him from moving as the eldritch stick-man crept up to stand next to his bed and leaned down.

As the great faceless head came into view Sir Richard finally managed to break the spell he was under, screaming in terror and lunging desperately from the bed to land on the floor, tangled amongst his bed-sheets.

"What? What's the matter?" Jacob had come instantly awake and stood, dagger held defensively before him, gaze darting around the room for signs of an attack before looking down at his master on the floor.

"Lord God Almighty!" Sir Richard gasped, his eyes wide, staring at the door which was firmly shut, the latch still locked in place. "God Almighty!" he repeated, making no effort to stand but grasping the hilt of his sword and holding it against his chest which rose and fell as if he'd been running. "A dream," he mumbled to his worried sergeant-at-arms. "Just a dream, although a very...very vivid one. Go back to sleep."

He climbed back into bed and rearranged the

thin covers over himself, the fear fading slowly as his brain accepted the fact there was no hellish stick-figure in the room and it had all been nothing more than a nightmare. Eventually he slumped back onto the pillow, praying to God that the dream wouldn't return.

* * *

The morning dawned, bright and sunny as it almost always was on Rhodes to the chagrin of the English Hospitallers who wished for a bit of rain to cool the air a little.

Father Vitus apologised for his absence the previous night and asked how things had gone with their investigation around the village. Sir Richard told him about their pursuit of the black-eyed man and the subsequent fatal fight in the apparently deserted settlement as the bearded little priest listened, his face screwed up in consternation.

"I have no idea where that place is," he told them, shaking his head in puzzlement. "There's nowhere within running distance that fits your description. There are little villages nearby of course, but none that sound like your description to me. Why no one was around is a mystery."

"Another one," Jacob grunted, biting into the soft white bread Athenais had provided for them.

"Indeed," the priest inclined his head with a tight smile as Sir Richard produced the piece of parchment he'd taken from the dead man the previous night.

"I can speak a little Greek, but I can't read it," the knight said, handing the parchment over for Father Vitus to inspect.

The puzzled look on his face changed to one of undisguised fear and the knight leaned forward to grip his wrist. "What does it say?"

"Nothing, it's nonsense," the priest replied, trying to snatch his hand away but Sir Richard held it in a vice-like grip and glared at him.

"Don't lie to me, priest! If you don't tell me what it says someone else will!"

Father Vitus returned the bearded knight's angry gaze but finally relented. "Have you heard of the Vrahnas?"

The Hospitallers looked at each other and shook their heads.

"The Vrahnas is a demon that comes to people in the night, as they sleep," Vitus told them his voice low, fearful, and Sir Richard felt his blood run cold.

"That's what it says on the parchment?" he demanded.

The little priest shook his head. "No. The Vrahnas has been...visiting...people since time began. It has many different names in the cultures of the world from what I understand, but it's basically the same thing." He stopped, licking his lips before taking a sip of the fruit juice in his cup. "The parchment here," he held it up, the sunlight streaming in through the open window showing the writing in stark contrast, "it says, 'Ο Ντάγκον έρχεται'... In your language that means 'Dagon is coming'."

Sir Richard's fingers tightened spasmodically

around his own wooden cup and the hairs on the back of his neck prickled as he replayed the scene from last night's dream in his head. The whispered chant he could hear in his head; he remembered it now. "Arra...arra...arra...Dagon...Dagon...Dagon..."

"Dagon has taken the place of the Vrahnas," Father Vitus continued, not noticing the knight's nervous reaction. "Only, where the Vrahnas frightened people...well, no one died. It was just a nightmare. Dagon though...when he visits he either sends his victim insane with terror or... there have been a lot of people dying in their sleep since tales of this devil started to circulate a while ago. Why his name was written on the parchment your attackers carried I can't say, but this is a warning. A curse! You must leave here now, forget this foolish investigation."

Jacob had watched his master's reaction to Father Vitus's information and now he spoke up. "You saw him last night, didn't you? This Dagon, or succubus or incubus or whatever the hell it is. That's why you were rolling about on the floor!"

Sir Richard's hand strayed to his sword hilt as he nodded a reply. "Aye. The demon came to me in my sleep," he admitted, looking at the priest for his reaction. "I couldn't move, couldn't even open my mouth to scream. Yet...when I managed to roll out of the bed and waken myself, there was no one there but Jacob and I."

"He was here?" Father Vitus looked interested rather than shocked or frightened. "Dagon was in the church buildings?"

"It was just a dream," Sir Richard smiled,

20

helping himself to some spiced pork. "I haven't been driven insane and I'm still very much alive. I'm sure it was more the result of the cheese I ate before I retired than any ancient demon trying to kill me."

The priest nodded and mumbled what sounded like a prayer of protection although the Hospitaller couldn't make out the words.

Athenais, the housekeeper, came in to clear the plates from the table and, as before, the knight noticed the priest casting surreptitious glances at her and he guessed Jacob wasn't the only one that was smitten by the girl's beauty.

"Douse that in holy water and burn it," Sir Richard stood, pointing grimly at the cursed parchment in Father Vitus's hand. "Jacob and I are going to the market to question the locals about this whole damn mystery. It'll take more than a bad dream to stop our investigation."

* * *

The morning was spent in the market, the bright sunlight reflecting off the hard ground and making the heat almost unbearable for the two English Hospitallers. The canopied stalls offered some respite but it was stifling even in the shade and the locals seemed to have – or admitted to – little knowledge of the disappearances in the area. The mention of the Vrahnas, or Dagon, the stick figure that haunted dreams, only resulted in the superstitious locals clamming up, wide-eyed with fear.

They bought a lunch of fruit, meat and cheese, although the cheese was warm and unpleasant to the Englishmen's' palates and Sir Richard regretted eating it as he recalled his earlier nightmare. A few cups of wine helped them digest the food but eventually, Sir Richard grew tired of the stifling heat and led them back to St Luke's, downcast and wondering how they'd ever get anywhere with this investigation if the locals wouldn't co-operate.

When they got back to the church buildings it was early evening and a young family were talking to Father Vitus. After a while Athenais led the small group off and the priest came across to talk to the Hospitallers who had waited by the front door to speak to him.

"Visitors?" Sir Richard wondered.

The priest nodded. "Travellers from the city. They're going to visit family on the far end of the island and sought a place to stay for the night. A bed here costs a lot less than a bed at an inn." He shrugged and fixed Sir Richard with an accusatory look. "Many people on the island are poor."

The knight knew Father Vitus was suggesting the Hospitallers persecuted and held down the Orthodox Christians on the island but he was experienced enough not to rise to the bait.

"We're getting nowhere with the villagers – no one wants to offer any information and it's obvious they're all afraid of this cult or whatever it is."

"Maybe," the Greek nodded. "Or maybe they just don't know anything."

"Whatever. We'll go out again at night and see if we can find a lead, but I expect we'll be back early."

* * *

Sir Richard's words proved prophetic and the Hospitallers were back in their room in St Luke's long before midnight. The locals proved just as unhelpful at night as they had during the oppressively hot day – more so in fact, as the absence of sunlight made the atmosphere appear even more threatening. So they returned to the church dejectedly and, after a frugal supper of bread and boiled eggs that they found in the little kitchen – presumably left out by the housekeeper who, like Father Vitus was nowhere to be seen – they said their evening prayers and climbed into their beds.

"I'll sleep with one eye open," Jacob said to his master as they lay in the humid darkness awaiting sleep. "If you dream of the Vrahnas, or Dagon, or anything like that, just grunt and I'll wake you up."

Sir Richard laughed softly. "I'll try," he replied. "It's not as easy as you'd think – when the dream came to me I was pinned down and couldn't move a muscle, even the ones in my mouth. Go to sleep and don't worry about me though, I'm sure my sleep will be fine tonight."

The scream roused Jacob a while later. Only a small sliver of moonlight illuminated the room but it was just enough for the sergeant-at-arms to find his master and roughly shake him to try and break the

23

nightmare he feared Sir Richard was trapped inside.

"Alright, alright!" The knight shoved Jacob's hands away. "What are you doing you madman?"

"I heard a cry," Jacob replied, lifting his sword that stood by his own bed and pulling it from its leather and wood sheath. "It woke me up. I assumed it was you."

Sir Richard lay his head back down on the straw mattress in exhaustion. "I think you're the one that's having bad dreams tonight," he muttered. "Maybe the eggs disagreed with you."

"I don't think it was a nightmare," Jacob shook his head. "Something definitely woke me..."

He stopped in mid-sentence and looked across at Sir Richard who had sat bolt-upright in the blackness as another pained cry filtered through their thick wooden door.

The knight jumped from the bed, grasping his own blade and ordered Jacob to follow him as they unlatched the door and cautiously made their way into the corridor outside their room.

The stone floor was surprisingly cold and both men felt the hairs on the back of their necks rise as they stared into the inky darkness of St Luke's.

"Help me!"

The scream allowed Sir Richard to get his bearings and he led his sergeant along the corridor, towards the room Athenais had taken the family from earlier to.

"Help me, please help me!"

The voice – a woman's – came again and this time they heard children's voices adding to the noise.

"There!" Jacob pointed at a sliver of light that

was shining from under a doorway in front of them. "It's coming from in there."

Sir Richard tried to open the door but it was locked from inside, so he hammered the pommel of his sword against the door. "Open up! Open the door in the name of Christ!"

Again there was another scream, this time coming from the woman and all the children that were inside the room and the Hospitaller had had enough.

"Stand back!" he roared. "Get away from the door, we're coming in!"

Without waiting for a reply Sir Richard leaned backwards, lifted his right leg and rammed his foot against the thick door, just beside the latch.

The wood held up but the latch was flimsy and, with a crack of splitting metal the door burst open and the knight moved carefully into the room, his longsword held defensively before him as Jacob following at his back, his own blade held at the ready.

"What's going on in here?" the knight demanded, eyes searching the room for any threat but finding nothing obvious.

The terrified woman pointed at her husband who lay on the bed, unmoving, and Sir Richard shuddered slightly at the expression on the man's face. He was clearly dead, although there didn't appear to be a wound on him, but his eyes were open and his expression was frozen in one of sheer terror.

The children cried and hid their faces against their mother's side, her thin arms squeezing them protectively as the tears streaked her tired face.

Jacob moved around the room, searching for an

enemy as Sir Richard asked, more gently this time, what had happened to the man.

"He began groaning in his sleep," she replied, her voice almost cracking. "It woke me up and I tried to shake him awake but he just kept making that noise, getting louder and louder. Then..." She stopped, shaking fearfully, "his eyes opened and he screamed as if he could see something in the room. I thought he must be dreaming – having a nightmare – but I turned to show him there was nothing there and..."

"Devil!" one of the children cried out, little knuckles white as he gripped his mother's arm, "the Devil was here – it killed our daddy!"

Sir Richard and Jacob glanced at each other, both thinking the same thing: Dagon.

Father Vitus appeared in the doorway, his dark eyes calmly taking in the scene before he moved across to the family and, kneeling beside them, began the Lord's Prayer in an attempt to comfort them. "Pater imon, o en tis ouranis, aghiasthito to onoma sou; eltheto i vasilia sou; ghenithito to thelima sou, os en ourano, ke epi tis ghis..."

"The devil *was* here," the Greek woman nodded tearfully over the drone of Father Vitus's voice. "Huge and thin he was, like a horrible insect without any face, and he..." She broke down again as she looked across at her dead husband's terror-stricken face. "He did that! On holy ground too, how could this happen!"

Sir Richard and Jacob examined the dead man as the little priest tried to soothe the angry, terrified woman, but they could find no visible cause of death.

Eventually, the Hospitaller closed the man's eyelids respectfully and made the sign of the cross, saying a silent prayer for his soul.

"Whatever happened," the knight straightened up and addressed the priest and the frightened, grieving woman, "there's no devil here now. We're sorry for your loss, and if we can do anything to help, you have but to ask. Come, Jacob, let's return to our room and leave these people alone to grieve."

The sound of Father Vitus's calm prayers followed them along the corridor as they returned to their room. Sir Richard shook his head, imagining he could detect a note of triumph – or perhaps it was pleasure – in the little Greek's voice.

* * *

The Hospitallers didn't sleep much for the rest of the night. A strange thumping noise seemed to fill the air outside periodically, apparently coming from somewhere nearby yet deep underground. Sir Richard knew there must be a prosaic explanation for the noise – a local mine working through the night perhaps – but the unearthly sound was unsettling, particularly for the superstitious Jacob, and especially after the events of earlier.

As the pair made their way to the small dining area in the morning they quietly discussed what might await them. Athenais was there, and she'd laid on a large but simple breakfast for the two soldiers, but when Sir Richard tried to find out what was happening with the bereaved family the girl simply shrugged her slim shoulders and said she didn't know anything about it.

"That little bastard's got her scared," Jacob growled when the girl left the room to complete the rest of her duties around the house.

Sir Richard offered no reply. Athenais did seem somewhat subdued around them, and Father Vitus's veiled looks whenever he saw her suggested there might be some truth to his sergeant's fears but, well, it was nothing to do with them. They were here to find out why three of their brothers had disappeared, not to get involved in the relationship between the priest and his housekeeper, whatever it might be.

They finished their meal with no sign of the family or Father Vitus – to Sir Richard's annoyance, as he'd wanted to question the priest in detail about the night's events – and so they left the church to continue their investigation at the local market, hoping for more success than they'd enjoyed the day before.

"You, sir! My lord!" A trader spied them as they wandered around the dusty streets, smile bright against his dark complexion, ingratiating and false as he hurried over in the hope of making a sale. "You look like men who have seen much evil. I have just the thing you need!" He opened his grubby jacket to reveal an assortment of poor quality jewellery. "Any of these will bring you good luck and protect you from harm. A man like you surely needs protection from the forces of darkness!" He gazed at Sir Richard slyly and the knight was struck by the man's pupils which were unnaturally dark given the bright sun that blazed overhead.

"You're right," the Hospitaller agreed, to the disgust of Jacob who grunted loudly, surprised that his master would be taken in by the shoddy pieces the seller was hawking. "I've seen many wicked, evil things in my time as a soldier. What's your name?"

"Leontios, my lord," the trader replied, moving in closer as Sir Richard continued in a low, conspiratorial tone.

"Most of my brother knights could use the protection you offer," the knight nodded. "Are these charms powerful?"

The man grinned, trying to conceal his glee at the knight's gullibility. "Sire, these may look like any other piece of high-quality jewellery for sale in the market, but" – he peered around as if he expected someone to be listening to their conversation before continuing – "these are endowed with powerful magic. It's perhaps better you don't know where their power comes from, but you can be sure they'll defend you against the devil and his many servants. I promise you, as a Christian man myself!"

"How much?" Sir Richard asked. "Not just for one of your stunning pieces, but for, say, ten, that I may give as gifts to some of the other Hospitallers?"

The seller practically rubbed his hands as he realised this English knight with the eight-pointed cross emblazoned on his red surcoat was ready to pay whatever price he demanded in return for his worthless pieces of glass. "Well, my lord" – he began, the sentence tailing off as Sir Richard produced his coin purse and emptied a sizeable amount of silver into his palm. "I would say" –

"What do you know of Dagon, Leontios?" the Hospitaller growled, looking into the eyes of the trader who found it hard to tear his gaze from the small fortune in the knight's hand. "And the disappearances that have been plaguing the area? Rest assured," he muttered into the man's ear, "none will know of your help in this. I simply seek information. And...if your information proves valuable to me I have gold as well as silver back in our citadel..."

The trader pondered the situation for a moment before reaching out for the silver coins in Sir Richard's hand, the lure of the money proving greater than any reticence he shared with the other market-goers at talking about the dark folklore of the island.

"I know much," he promised, glaring at Sir Richard who pulled the handful of coins out of reach of his grasping fingers.

"Then tell me! Where can I find these people?" Too fast for the eye to follow, a dagger appeared in the Hospitaller's hand and the trader shrank back as the point pressed against his windpipe, Jacob moving in at his back to stop him moving out of reach. "Your choice. Hospitaller silver filling your pockets or my steel in your windpipe."

The man glared at him before he dropped his eyes to the money still held invitingly in the Hospitaller's left hand. He looked up, the ingratiating smile again painted across his odd face and he nodded in acquiescence.

"I'll show you where to find the men you seek."

* * *

"This is the way we came last night, chasing that man from the market," Jacob noted as they left the busy village and moved into the countryside. "I remember passing those houses on the outskirts; one of them had a strange symbol painted on a flat stone beside it; like a line with five smaller lines branching off it."

Sir Richard nodded agreement. "I remember it too." His hand strayed to his weapon. "Be ready for another ambush, although I'm pretty sure this guide of ours is more interested in our money than seeing us dead."

They moved at a steady pace for a while, passing through open countryside until they saw a small settlement in the near-distance, bordered by fields in which the locals, presumably, grew crops.

As they walked, Sir Richard looked at his sergeant, noticing Jacob's gaze fixed on something in the field they were passing. The knight squinted, trying to see what had attracted his man's attention, although the harsh bright sunshine made it difficult for him to see. "What is it?" he muttered.

Jacob's eyes never left the point on which they were focused as he replied. "A man. In the field, there."

Sir Richard finally spotted the figure that had captivated his sergeant. It was a man with in a wide-brimmed hat some distance away, wearing long trousers and a long-sleeved red coat despite the heat, and he was returning their stare.

The man never moved at all as the Hospitallers and their guide walked past, just standing, still like a statue, only his head seeming to turn slightly as he kept the travellers in sight.

"He's been stood there without moving the whole time," Jacob said. "Just watching us pass by."

Sir Richard made the sign of the cross, unsettled by the malevolent figure's lack of movement.

"That's not a man," their guide waved a hand dismissively, listening to their conversation. "It's a straw man. Farmers use them to frighten birds away. Have you never seen one before?"

"A straw man!" Sir Richard laughed, slapping his sergeant on the back with a grin. "Well, that would explain why it's not bloody moving! Come on, Jacob, you're jumping at shadows here, let's get a move on."

They continued at a greater pace, the knight trying to engage their Greek guide in conversation about the local disappearances without success.

Jacob turned to the field again just as they entered the village they'd been in the previous evening. "Straw man is it, eh?" he growled. "Fastest fucking straw man I've ever seen then."   ·

Sir Richard and Leontios looked back over their shoulders and the Hospitaller again made the sign of the cross.

The figure was gone.

    * * *

32

"What's the name of this place?" Sir Richard asked. "We were here last night, but the priest that's putting us up couldn't think where it was when we described it to him."

"Krymmeni Thesi," the guide replied, giving the knight an unfathomable look. "I don't know why the priest couldn't tell you that: everyone knows this place. It's been here for aeons. "

Aeons. Odd choice of word Sir Richard thought, looking around at the little village. This time there were people – locals – in the streets or sitting outside the ramshackle little stone houses, watching with suspicious glares as they passed.

"I'll leave you here now." Their guide suddenly stopped, his hand stretched out towards Sir Richard, looking for payment for his services.

"You'll leave no-one, yet," the big knight retorted, his eyes burning, despite the control in his voice. "You've brought us here, but we need to find the men that are behind the disappearances. You'll take us to them, as agreed, and then we'll see about your payment."

The Greek's face grew angry, but it was clear he wouldn't see any more silver unless he fulfilled his promise. "All right, my lords," he shrugged. "Follow me."

The man walked off, at a brisk pace, towards the eastern side of Krymmeni Thesi.

Soon they came into sight of what appeared to be an excavation by the side of the road, touching on the land adjoining a run-down, apparently unoccupied house. The three men halted at the sight of the crudely armed guards, as Leontios didn't want to be seen by them.

"That's where you need to go," their guide told them. "Not those men," he clarified, waving a hand dismissively. "The leaders are underground, in the tunnels those fools are guarding. Now..." he grinned wolfishly at Sir Richard, holding his hands out expectantly.

"Fair enough," the knight agreed. "I'll pay you this for the moment." He handed the guide a few small silver coins. "If your information proves useful I'll seek you out at the market and quadruple that!"

The man turned with a smile and hurried off the way they had come as the Hospitaller shouted after him. "How did you know these men were here?"

"Everyone knows," the guide threw back over his shoulder. "They're just too frightened to say or do anything about it."

"Then why aren't *you* too frightened..."

The Greek ignored the question, picking up pace until he was out of sight amongst the houses lining the road and Jacob snorted.

"Men like him don't feel fear; not when there's a coin to be made."

"Well, whatever his motives," the knight replied, moving towards the swarthy, weather-beaten men standing around the ruined tunnel entrance, "he brought us where we wanted to be. Let's see what we can find here."

The men remained lounging against the ancient, low sandstone wall that formed a crescent around the stairs leading down to the tunnel but the Hospitallers' trained eyes noticed the slight stiffening of limbs as they prepared themselves either for fight or flight.

"What can we do for you knights of the cross?" the eldest of the men asked, his face set in a scowl. Presumably this was the foreman. His pupils were so big that they obscured the iris and, looking at the rest of the guards Sir Richard realised all had the same sinister black eyes. *They must eat some strange mushroom or something else native to Rhodes that makes them go like that,* he thought, unconsciously raising his hand to touch the crucifix he wore around his neck.

"For starters, you can stand aside," he growled, "so my sergeant and I can take a look down there."

"You can't!" One of the guards raised his shovel threateningly towards them.

The foreman waved an angry hand for the worker to be silent. "Forgive this man's...exuberance," he growled to Sir Richard. "He speaks truly, though. You can't go down there – it's a religious site."

"I don't give a damn if it's the Garden of Gethsemane," Jacob replied, moving forward to place his face in front of the Greek foreman's. "We're going down there, whether you like it or not."

The other workers – four of them – stood up, hefting the spades and brushes they'd apparently been using to keep the stairway clear of sand, obviously prepared to use violence to stop these two invaders from entering their tunnel.

"My sergeant's right," Sir Richard spoke into the strained silence, the authority in his voice lending an air of much-needed calm to proceedings. "We *are* going down there. Whether you let us pass now, or whether we have to return with fifty fully armed

Hospitaller knights to force our way inside...it's up to you. But if I return with more of my brethren I'll make sure this place is brought down about your ears." He moved forward to stand beside Jacob, and glared at the furious foreman. "We're the authority on this island now, so you'd better get used to it. Now...what's it to be?"

He placed his weight on his left leg and calmly drew his sword while Jacob followed his master's lead with a smile.

"Why do you want to go down? What d'you think's down there?"

"We were told this place might have something to do with the Hospitallers that disappeared recently," Sir Richard replied. "I give you my word as a Christian: when we go in we'll treat the place with the respect it deserves."

For a short time the foreman stood, apparently mulling over his limited options, the workmen at his back still bristling with the potential for violence.

"Go," he finally told them. "But be quick. You'll not find what you're looking for, though, you're wasting your time."

"My thanks to you." The Hospitaller bowed slightly in gratitude and walked past him, sheathing his sword as he went down the stairs and through the heavy wooden door that lay slightly ajar, Jacob following at his back.

Inside was a simple antechamber lit by torches which led into the gently sloping tunnel they walked along now, senses straining for signs of danger, or any clue as to what this place might be used for. The air in the tunnel was cool, but there was an unnerving smell which the two men couldn't place. It told of ancient decay and unnameable horror, as if from some long-forgotten memory, and it made the hairs on the back of Sir Richard's neck stand up as they moved deeper into the claustrophobic darkness.

Some of the walls bore crude carvings, showing strange animals or insects which the Englishmen couldn't recognize; indeed, the carvings seemed to show beings that didn't look like they belonged to this world at all, but the guttering torches that hung on the walls were few and far between and it was difficult to make out much detail in the stone depictions.

"My God, I hope we don't meet that thing down here," Jacob murmured, eyeing one bas-relief that depicted some great tentacled beast towering over buildings and the people that prostrated themselves beneath it.

The sergeant turned to look at Sir Richard as he let out a small gasp which echoed along the fetid corridor.

"Dagon."

The knight was gazing at an eye-level carving, shadows from the flickering torchlight making it almost seem to move of its own accord. It depicted a tall, humanoid figure with obscenely long legs, arms and even fingers that appeared to be engaged in the act of stealing a small child from its screaming, yet unresisting family.

"We're not going to find anything down here," Sir Richard mumbled, tearing his eyes away from the bas-relief. "Look at these pictures: every one of them has the moon or stars in the background. Whatever this twisted religion is, it prefers night time. Come on," he pushed past Jacob and headed back along the tunnel towards the big wooden entrance door. "We'll get some rest and come back here later tonight. Perhaps we'll be able to see exactly what these people get up to when the stars wheel overhead and they think no-one's watching them..."

* * *

The Hospitallers had left the tunnel, apologising to the workmen they'd disturbed – Sir Richard even giving the glowering foreman a small donation of silver for their trouble – and made their way back to St Luke's to await dusk. The family of the man who had died in his sleep had gone to stay with relatives according the Father Vitus, leaving his body in the care of the priest to be prepared for the funeral. The Greek quizzed them on their investigation's progress but the knight gave nothing away, simply asking for a meal and some wine before he and Jacob retired to their room for a nap.

They awoke refreshed and ready for their night's work in Krymmeni Thesi. The sun was just setting, its red light throwing sinister shadows across the buildings outside the Hospitaller's bedroom window as they climbed through it into the street rather than alerting Father Vitus to their movements.

Sir Richard didn't believe the priest had anything to do with the disappearances or the strange religion that apparently operated out of the tunnel in Krymmeni Thesi, but he didn't see any reason to tell the secretive little man where they were going tonight. The less people that knew, the better.

That said, the big knight mused, scratching his beard as they jogged through the street, *our guide from earlier seemed to think Vitus* must *have known about Krymmeni Thesi. So why didn't he tell us when we asked about it?*

It was a question for another day – they had enough to worry about that night.

They reached the village soon enough; thankfully the strange figure that had been standing in the field observing them earlier in the day hadn't returned. Sir Richard didn't want the volatile Jacob chasing through a field, sword drawn, to deal with the 'straw man'.

No, the journey was uneventful, although the very air again seemed charged with negative, oppressive energy. Two normal men might have given up and gone home, but the Hospitallers had seen, and done, much fighting for Christ. The idea of devils and demons wasn't enough to stop Sir Richard's investigation.

The houses stood silent and unlit, just as they had the previous night when the Hospitallers had fought and killed two of the black-eyed men. The unearthly, threatening atmosphere that had followed them ever since they'd left St Luke's became almost unbearable as the two soldiers walked silently towards the tunnel entrance they'd visited earlier in the day.

The five workmen from earlier – the very same ones from the look of them – still stood on guard at the top of the stairs, although Sir Richard growled at their incompetence as they again lounged about the low, ancient stone wall that marked the staircase down to the tunnel.

As they watched from the shadows a couple, dressed in dark hooded robes approached the entrance, showed something they wore around their necks to the guards and were waved down and through the entrance without a word passing between any of them.

"Interesting," Sir Richard muttered to his sergeant. "If we had a couple of those amulets or whatever that was they had we might be able to just walk straight through. But, since we haven't," he stood up, beckoning Jacob to follow, "we need a diversion to get them away from the entrance."

Jacob shook his head. "A diversion? What for? They might outnumber us but they're just farmers and labourers. We can take them."

Sir Richard crept away to a nearby house, gesturing his sergeant to follow.

"We can't just walk up and butcher them," he replied. "We have no proof they're doing anything wrong and you can be sure their foreman told his superiors that we were sniffing around earlier. If they were all to die violently, without any hard evidence of wrong-doing, the locals will go crazy and the Grand Master'll have our heads." He halted, peering into the windows of the house, checking no one was around. "Make sure no one appears from a side street like they did before."

Jacob drew his sword and peered around at the darkness, vowing not to be blind-sided again as Sir Richard drew out his tinderbox and struck flint against steel. There was a wooden outhouse with some damaged old furniture in it attached to the main building and with the suffocating climate on the island it was simple enough to set it alight.

"Come on!"

Jacob followed his master's lead back to the tunnel entrance just as the guards caught the smell of burning in the air.

"What's that?" one of them asked, sniffing loudly. "You smell that?"

The Hospitaller's couldn't fully understand what was being said as the Greeks spoke excitably but the gist of the conversation was obvious and the alarm apparent as the slowly building fire became large enough to cast an orange glow in the sky.

The men began to hurry over to extinguish the blaze before it got out of hand and Sir Richard grinned in satisfaction.

Then there was a shout and the guards halted in their tracks. The foreman berated them, pointing down at the stairs leading to the tunnel. There was some heated argument then, particularly by one guard but the foreman ran over and punched the dissenter hard in the face, knocking him back against the low wall.

The rest of the guardsmen lowered their heads, muttering under their breaths in anger, but they followed their leader's directions and walked back to their positions in front of the tunnel entrance.

Clearly it was more important to make sure no uninvited guests went into the tunnel than it was to extinguish a fire that could, potentially, destroy the whole village.

"They're leaving it to burn!" Jacob muttered in disbelief. "By all that's holy, whatever they're protecting down there must be important..."

Sir Richard nodded in exasperation. Clearly their ruse wasn't going to work. "Draw your weapon," he ordered, pulling his own fine longsword from its leather sheath. "Looks like we'll have to try your direct route after all."

Whereas the Hospitallers had travelled with only light clothing earlier in the day, they now wore full chain-mail, covered by the red surcoats with white eight pointed star of their Order proudly emblazoned on the front. They wore no helmets, knowing the darkened conditions and possible close-combat they'd be faced with would only be made more difficult by a heavy lump of steel the wearer could barely see out of.

"Who's that?" The voice was that of the foreman. He didn't sound worried, or frightened by the sight of two shadowy figures approaching, just surprised. "Who's that?" he repeated, louder, when he didn't get a reply.

Sir Richard and Jacob held their swords behind their backs so the torches that guttered by the tunnel entrance, and the fire they'd set – which was already beginning to burn itself out – wouldn't reflect off their blades and warn the workmen of their impending doom.

They approached the guards who stood up, knowing something was obviously wrong, and the Hospitallers roared their battle-cries into the charred air of the ghost town.

Sir Richard thrust the point of his longsword

down and into the thigh of the first worker to engage him. The man collapsed, screaming in shock as thick blood spurted from the fatal wound which he tried to close, uselessly, with a shaking hand.

Without slowing, the knight brought his blade round and up by his right shoulder, ready to swing it down into the head of his next target. The guard instinctively dodged to the left, thinking he was a step ahead of the big Hospitaller but before he could aim a blow of his own he felt the boot of Sir Richard battering into the side of his knee and he collapsed instantly.

The knight's blade was thrust into the guard's heart and, as the man died, Sir Richard looked up to see his sergeant-at-arms fighting off the remaining three men.

One of them was crouching, bleeding profusely from a terrible wound across the midriff, so the knight jumped forward and ran the point of his sword into the man's face which exploded in a spray of blood and bone while Jacob dispatched another with a thrust to the heart.

The foreman panicked as he realized he was the last of his comrades still standing. He half-ran, half-fell down the stairs to raise the alarm but Sir Richard had guessed his intentions and was able to reach him before he hauled the door open, slamming the man's head against the stone wall before impaling him on his sword.

"Now," the Knight of Rhodes grunted into the inky darkness, breathing heavily after the exertion, "we find out what these people are doing down there."

Again, as it had before, the stench of decay and some half-remembered damp horror pervaded the air of the tunnel and Sir Richard began to think of it as more of a tomb.

This time, though, there was something else in the air: the sound of a large number of people congregated and chanting together as one. The Hospitallers couldn't make out the words through the dark caverns so they slowly made their way along the tunnel again as they had previously, only this time they held their bloodied swords defensively before them, ready for whatever this unholy place might throw at them.

They passed the blasphemous wall-carvings, trying not to look too closely as the sound of chanting grew louder and the walls seemed to close in around them. Every so often one of the Hospitallers would turn with a low cry as they heard a footstep behind them or a whispered laugh in their ear, but they could see nothing in the gloom and the knight assumed it was some trick of the tunnel's construction that was causing the sounds.

Eventually, Sir Richard grasped his sergeant by the arm, slowing their progress as the passage gave way onto a great cavern lit by dozens of torches and they spotted another guard, his back turned to them. It was a measure of their anxiety that the Hospitallers were glad to see a human enemy standing in the tunnel.

"There may be more of them," the knight whispered, gesturing Jacob back into a shadowy alcove in the tunnel wall.

The pair stood and watched to get an idea of the guard's routine, if any, or if there were any more of the silent watchers. The chanting continued and, although it was meaningless to the Christian Hospitallers, the words became recognizable eventually.

"Arra, Arra, Arra, Dagon, Dagon, Dagon..."

The chant repeated over and over and, despite its obviously blasphemous intent, Sir Richard found the refrain hypnotic and he stood, spellbound for long moments until Jacob nudged him gently.

"What do we do now?"

Sir Richard looked at him in confusion before the realisation of where they were came back to him and he motioned forward.

"We remove that guard and see for ourselves what the hell's going on in that cavern."

They padded forward, the chant masking any sound they might have made, and the knight grasped the guard from behind, bringing his dagger around, slicing it deep across the man's throat, sending a spurt of blood showering over the blade.

It's hungry tonight, Sir Richard thought, smiling at his blade before he caught himself in disgust, wondering where such a monstrous notion had come from. The chant, the cavern, the ancient obscene bas-reliefs...it was enough to send a man mad.

Jacob had moved to deal with the only other guard that seemed to be around, silencing him quickly with a sword thrust to the kidney and a couple of cracks on the skull with his pommel. He crossed back to stand with his master and they gazed down on the scene below, the chants of "Arra! Dagon!" filling the huge cavern as they rose in intensity.

"Look," Sir Richard growled, pointing to two separate places behind the great stone altar.

Jacob squinted into the gloomy haze beneath them, trying to see what his master had spotted before his eyes widened in anger.

Three red surcoats bearing white, eight-pointed crosses, hung from long poles like trophies.

"At least we know what happened to our brothers," the knight muttered, before he shrank back out of the light as something seemed to be happening at last beneath them.

A figure at the rear of the room, well-lit by the large candles and torches on the altar before it although its face was hidden by a crude mask, stepped forward and raised its arms to the worshipping throng which seemed to hold its collective breath reverentially.

Silence reigned for long moments and, as time extended, Sir Richard felt the uncontrollable urge to cough.

He looked at Jacob, staring at him in horror, his face turning scarlet, fists clenched tightly, but at last the knight couldn't hold it in any longer, even though it would give them away to the gathered worshippers and he opened his mouth, a hacking cough bursting from his lips.

"Welcome!" The priest shouted, raising his arms and the gathered mass of people gleefully returned his greeting, filling the cavern with their voices.

Offering a grateful prayer of thanks to God the Hospitallers settled down to watch proceedings as the priest continued his oration in Greek. Occasionally the people replied in kind, obviously well-versed in whatever black mass this whole event constituted but the two Englishmen couldn't keep up and had no idea what was going on.

Eventually the congregation took up the "Arra! Arra! Arra! Dagon! Dagon! Dagon!" chant again, this time with even more enthusiasm, the syllables cascading horrifically around the ceiling of the centuried cavern. A movement off to the side caught the watchers' eyes and they stared in shock as a young couple were dragged through the throng who shouted and laughed in joy as the man and woman passed, crying and screaming as they went.

"Surely not," Jacob growled. "Human sacrifice?"

Sir Richard watched as the couple were led to the altar and a large man approached them. He struck each of them brutally on the forehead with some knobbed cudgel and their protestations ended instantly as they slumped, either dead or unconscious, onto the floor.

It always amazed the Hospitaller knight when he saw people die in front of a crowd. This was the first time he'd been witness to a human sacrifice, but he'd seen plenty of hangings, beheadings and even more inhumane executions in the name of justice. Always, without exception, the normal people there to witness it – men, women and children alike –

47

became so carried away at the sight of someone else's suffering that they'd scream and cheer and sing and make merry as if it were Yuletide. And when it was over, and the unfortunate victim was swinging from a gibbet, the people would head home – happy at their day's excitement.

This, though...this was a level beyond that. The crazed chant reverberated around the great room as the man with the cudgel stepped back to let the masked priest pass. The figure produced a long, wickedly curved knife and moved towards the first of the unconscious victims. He leaned down, running the blade across the man's throat methodically, as if the exact size and depth of the killing cut was somehow gravely important then, as the blood spilled from the horrific wound, he placed a cup underneath and collected it.

When the vessel could hold no more he stood up and placed it on the altar, producing another, similar cup from somewhere beneath the great stone monolith. He stood, as if catching his breath as the worshippers chanted and screamed in delight.

"Come on, we've seen enough," Sir Richard said, silently offering a prayer for the dying couple's souls before grabbing his sergeant-at-arms by the sleeve and heading back up the tunnel towards the main door.

"Eh? Aren't we going to help her?" Jacob demanded, staring in horror as the loathsome masked priest bent next to the girl who was just returning to consciousness, her eyes opened wide in terror as the face of her would-be killer swam into view.

"How the hell are we going to do that?" Sir

Richard shouted over his shoulder, running now, as if desperate to put as much distance between himself and the repugnant rite that was occurring in the cyclopean cavern behind them. "She's dead already! Now move, before they finish their filthy ceremony and start to head back to their homes!" Tears of rage and sorrow streamed down his face as he ran, sickened to be leaving the girl to her fate but knowing there was nothing he could do to save her.

"Where are we going?" Jacob demanded, hurrying to catch his master. "What are we going to do?"

"First, we get out of here," the knight replied. "Then we find Leontios – I have some questions for him. After that we'll head back to St Luke's and rest, before we take this news to the Grand Master in the morning."

They reached the front doors and, swords still in hand, burst through, ready for any attack.

None came.

The guards they'd killed earlier hadn't been discovered and the village lay enshrouded in silence. All was quiet, just as it had been when they entered the hateful tunnel a short time ago.

As they passed the field from earlier on that day neither man was surprised to see the 'straw man' had returned, watching in silence from the gloom as they passed.

* * *

"Flat stones?"

"Aye, Leontios, stones that bear some inscription. We've seen them dotted around the town. What are they?"

The Greek merchant's eyes flickered nervously around the market and he shrugged his shoulders but the Hospitaller knight grabbed him and slammed him against the sandstone wall.

"Don't play with me!" Sir Richard roared, his voice startlingly loud in the quiet of the evening despite the bustling of the market. "You know a lot about these heretics – devil-worshippers – you even have the black eyes they all share, which suggests to me you were one of them at some point if you're not still some agent of theirs. I believe the symbol we've seen painted on flat stones around the town is related to this Dagon and his followers. Tell me what you know about it, now, or by God I'll see you tried as one of them!"

The man sighed and Sir Richard softened his tone, surprised to see a tear spilling down the merchants face. "Tell me what I need to know, Leontios and I'll see you well rewarded."

The merchant nodded slowly, his expression unreadable as he pondered his options. "They… they gave us all a choice. Join them and reap the rewards when the Deep Ones return to reclaim their rightful place, or watch as our families die. I joined them but..." More tears streaked his face which twisted in anger as he continued. "My wife Alexis – a good Christian, incorruptible," he smiled, gazing into space, "refused. As I should have!"

There was silence for a while until Sir Richard

prodded the man to continue.

"They sacrificed her to Dagon."

The sounds of the market continued around them as Sir Richard and Jacob watched the Greek merchant relive his wife's death, the pain evident in his damp eyes.

"I vowed then to see them stopped, but I could do nothing by myself and could approach no-one for help. The villagers are too frightened to do anything for fear of losing their loved ones and, until you arrived, there seemed no way to stand against them. The religion only came to prominence recently, brought here from somewhere in Mesopotamia I've been told, but I believe their underground cavern to be much older than any of the Christian buildings on the island. You've seen those bas-reliefs – they depict scenes from a time long forgotten by any historian. And the Dagonites seek to bring those times back; to destroy Christian, Muslim and Jew alike so their evil god and his brethren can enslave us all!"

"I knew this was all true," Jacob mumbled fearfully. "I knew it..."

"Well, we're here now," Sir Richard said, throwing a murderous glance in his superstitious sergeant's direction, "and our Order won't allow these blasphemers to continue their evil ways, I can assure you. Tell us what we need to know to stop them."

Leontios nodded, hope flaring in his eyes. "They believe I'm still one of them; that's why I'm still alive. I discovered some wild mushrooms that, when ingested, make my pupils enlarge as theirs do when they...partake of Dagon's victims' blood...Don't ask me how it works, but it makes them insane – the

51

blood-lust carries even good people away into a vicious madness. They don't remember what they did when they awake in the morning back in their own beds."

"Is Father Vitus involved?" Sir Richard asked.

Again the merchant shrugged. "Almost everyone in the surrounding villages is involved in one way or another. But only those with black eyes are part of it; the rest do nothing through fear of retribution. It is said Dagon can enslave a soul, even in the afterlife." He shuddered before continuing in a small voice. "Father Vitus is, I believe, Dagon's high priest."

The knight was shocked by the man's assertion. It had become more and more apparent the Greek priest was involved, somehow, in the disappearances, but...high priest of Dagon? Nothing they'd seen in St Luke's suggested the man was so intimately involved in the twisted religion. His eyes were normal and when he prayed to God Sir Richard would have sworn the man was as devout in his Orthodox belief as the Hospitaller was in his own Catholicism. Sir Richard simply couldn't believe it.

The traders had packed away their wares by now and the market was silent around them and Leontios's face twisted in panic as he realised his collusion with the Hospitallers might be noted.

"Here, take this and sleep with it by your side." He pressed a small, flat stone into Sir Richard's gauntleted hand and the knight examined it curiously. It was inscribed with the symbol they'd seen on the house on the outskirts of the town; a line with five smaller lines branching off it, like a tree. "It'll protect you," the merchant promised, "as it protects the buildings you've seen with the same stones outside. I must go now – if they discover I'm helping you they'll kill me as they did my wife."

He pulled away from the knight's grasp and headed off into the shadows. "Come to me again if you need me. But act quickly – Dagon is coming!"

* * *

Sir Richard's rest was plagued by dreams and nightmares that night. Dagon appeared again, the paralysis that had held the knight fast to the bed previously returning along with the monstrous stick-figure, who stood looking down on him from its faceless head high above. The terrified Hospitaller tried desperately to reach for his blade, or stand up, or even just to scream, but he was held motionless against the bed as the monstrous figure leaned towards him.

The knight had been close to death many times before but facing your own doom while holding your sword in your hand like a man was nothing compared to the crushing, hopeless sense of terror he felt as Dagon reached out to tear his unresisting body apart. An image of his two young sons came to him and a wave of sadness engulfed him as he realised he'd never see them again; never teach them to wield a sword, fish in the Calder or ride a horse.

Suddenly, just as the horrific head and slender arms were about to take him, the apparition shrank back and stood, motionless. A moment later, the black figure left the room and the knight rose with a strangled, choking cry, clutching the inscribed stone Leontios had given him.

Praise be to God, it had worked. The stone had worked!

Relief flooded through him and after a time his breath slowed, his heartbeat returning to it's normal, steady rate until finally, exhausted, he began to drift back into sleep with a small smile on his lips.

Then the realisation hit him like a crossbow bolt to the guts. After everything that had happened over the past few days, it finally sank in, and his breath caught in his throat again.

This is really happening – Dagon is real! Jesus Christ Almighty, protect us...!

They made their way to the dining area in the morning to find Vitus and Athenais who handed them each a plate with bread, cheese and smoked meats and cups of cool water before bowing respectfully to the men – never meeting their eyes as usual – and leaving the room to perform whatever duties she had that day.

"How's your investigation going?" the priest asked, watching his housekeeper as she left and sitting down at the little table with them as they broke their fast.

Sir Richard shovelled a lump of bread into his mouth and looked the little man in the eyes. "We know what's happening to the people that are disappearing," he said. "And we're going to do something about it, just as soon as we finish this."

Vitus raised an eyebrow but clasped his hands as if offering a prayer of thanks to God. "Tell me, are these people dead?" he asked.

Jacob nodded his head vigorously, spilling water from his mouth as he washed down a slice of salted pork. "Dead as anyone's ever been," he said. "You should have seen it" –

"Enough!" Sir Richard growled. "We don't know if all the victims are dead," he said, glaring at his sergeant. "And it's probably just as well Father Vitus *didn't* see it." He turned his attention back to the Greek priest. "We'll be leaving as soon as we finish breakfast and will no longer have need of your hospitality, which we thank you for. You've been a good host."

"Thank Athenais for us too, if you would, father," Jacob nodded, eyeing the man grimly.

Vitus returned a thin smile. "I'll pass it on to her. I hope you can put an end to the evil that's roaming our streets."

"We'll see," the big knight replied, washing down a final mouthful of food as he stood up. "We'll see. Come on, Jacob. Time we returned to the fortress and reported our findings to the Grand Master."

* * *

"Here? On my island?" Foulques de Villaret asked, his eyes narrowed in disbelief. "Are you sure about this Richard?"

The English knight nodded, his bearded face

55

deadly serious. "I am, Grand Master. We saw the young man's throat being cut and it's obvious the girl was about to suffer the same fate as we left. The fact we could do nothing to help her will haunt me for the rest of my days. May God rest her soul."

De Villaret sat down heavily, head tilted back, gazing at the ceiling. "I'll not suffer devil worshippers on this island. We must put an end to this blasphemy."

Sir Richard nodded. "In God's name, we must."

The knight had omitted many of the details of the last few days. He hadn't mentioned his dreams or their sightings of the eldritch straw man in the field. Such anecdotes would merely make him and Jacob sound like hysterical children.

"Take thirty men," de Villaret said. "Brother-knight Jean de Pagnac will assist you; make up the rest from our mercenaries. It'll be good experience for them." He fixed Sir Richard with an earnest stare. "If you can – find out the purpose of the sacrifices. But if you can't, just *wipe them from the face of the Earth!*"

The Englishman nodded. "I will, Grand Master, in the name of God and St John."

He genuflected to his superior and left the chamber. A sergeant-at-arms spotted him as he walked and shouted for him to wait.

"There's been a man – a local – around asking for you this morning, sir," the sergeant told him. "Said you owed him money."

The knight grasped the man's arm. "Leontios," he murmured.

"Aye, that was the name he gave us. He'll probably be back again soon, if you want to speak to him."

Sure enough, the Greek merchant appeared outside the fortress a short time later, asking after Sir Richard. The knight shouted for the gate guards to let the informer inside and greeted the man with a small smile when they met in the courtyard.

"Leontios, you're taking a chance coming here."

"I had to," the man agreed. "They're planning another sacrifice – more than one – tonight. You must stop them. You don't understand the depth of their evil! The whole point of this – their sacrifices – is to bring Dagon back to life so he can resurrect the rest of his kind. Christ and all his saints are nothing compared to the power of the Deep Ones!"

Sir Richard nodded reassuringly, inwardly questioning the man's sanity. "You can rest easy," he said, patting Leontios's arm. "We're going in tonight. Whatever they're planning, we'll put a stop to it, I promise you. Your Alexis will be avenged."

"Then I can help you again," Leontios replied. "I know another way into their cavern..."

* * *

There were very few English Hospitallers on Rhodes at that time, so Sir Richard noticed the familiar Yorkshire accent straight away.

The voice belonged to another sergeant-at-arms, who seemed more than competent at his job as he shepherded the mercenaries under his command into line with the occasional foul-mouthed roar that seemed almost as blasphemous to Sir Richard as the actions of the devil-worshippers they sought to apprehend.

"I fucking give up," the sergeant growled, shaking his head as Sir Richard walked up to stand beside him, surveying the men they were to lead back to Krymmeni Thesi. "Useless farm boys most of 'em, and the rest are too old to wipe their own arses, never mind wield a sword properly. Of course, from the rumours going about the citadel, there's some monster hidden away in this village we've to visit. I can hold my own," he looked at Sir Richard, "but I don't think I've ever had to fight an ancient monster."

The big knight smiled, warming immediately to the bluff younger man. "Good to have you on board, sergeant. We didn't see any monsters back in that village, so you can put your mind – and those of your men – at rest. It's just a group of devil worshippers and blasphemers. But they're normal men that die like any other."

Jacob appeared, newly shaven and looking fresher than he had for days. "I see you've met Stephen," he smiled to Sir Richard, nodding at the other sergeant-at-arms. "Good Yorkshireman, he is. Just what we need for this job."

"A good Yorkshireman is what you need for *any* job," Stephen grunted a dour reply, but his eyes twinkled. "Don't worry though – my master, Sir Jean de Pagnac, is French, but he's a right hardy fighter. Between the four of us we'll be able to keep this lot – " he pointed his thumb at the inexperienced Hospitallers arrayed behind them "– in check, and boot the arses of these heretics."

The memory of the young man and women being brutally sacrificed in the enormous cavern came back to Sir Richard in a rush and he gripped his sword-hilt convulsively. "I hope so," he said. "That evil has to be eradicated and who better to do it than God's chosen Order? Mount up!" he roared. "The sun's setting; let's get this over with."

* * *

The journey to Krymmeni Thesi was a short one, mounted as the Hospitallers were on great warhorses. As they passed through the market near Father Vitus's church the people shrank back, pointing and muttering amongst themselves, wondering what was happening. Such a show of military force was unusual since the island had been taken over completely by the knights, so the locals knew something big was happening.

They soon left the town behind and reached the fields on the outskirts of their destination, lit by a near-full moon. The bizarre straw man figure was nowhere to be seen; in its place, a man in a wide-brimmed hat walked along with a watering pot, soaking the earth beneath although what plants he might be growing was a mystery to Sir Richard as the field looked like it contained nothing more than simple grass. The sight of a man ceaselessly watering grass with a heavy pot which he would periodically refill from a barrel was a strangely unsettling one, especially in the near-dark and the Hospitaller gripped the painted flat stone Leontios had given him the night before, angry at himself for trusting in protection other than the cross on his surcoat and shield.

The farmer never once looked up at them as they passed, nor did he modify his pace, stop to wipe his brow, or otherwise deviate from his task.

Even the grim sergeant-at-arms, Stephen, shook his head in relief when they'd left the unearthly solitary gardener behind.

As they rode into Krymmeni Thesi they were greeted again with the sight of an apparently deserted village. As before, no lights burned in the houses and no people walked the streets.

"You!" Sir Richard started in his saddle, surprised to notice a figure skulking behind the wall of a house. "Where do we find your headman? Where is he?"

The man moved out from his hiding place and gazed up at the knight, impressive in his well-maintained chain mail and red surcoat with its white cross, and screwed up his black eyes as the moonlight flooded them. "He?" the man asked in a thin, reedy voice before laughing and hurrying off towards the centre of the village.

The Hospitaller spat in disgust and waved his men forward, towards the tunnel entrance on the western edge of town.

When they reached it, Sir Richard and Jacob shared a confused look. A new foreman was there, obvious by his size and bearing, but so were four guards and, although it was dim in the moonlight so they couldn't have sworn to it, the two Englishmen thought some of them had been killed during the previous evening's fight.

It was dark though, Sir Richard thought, shrugging off the superstitious thoughts that crowded in on his already strained frame of mind. *A lot of these Greek men look alike.*

The foreman turned to face them as the heavily armed horsemen approached and Sir Richard noted he carried a sword and wore a gambeson. The rest of his men were similarly equipped. Clearly, the previous evening's events had resulted in a heightened sense of security at the tunnel entrance.

"What do you want, Hospitaller?" The foreman's hand was on his sword-hilt and he showed no sign of fear or deference as he glared up at the English knight. His men stood and formed a wall behind him, their eyes stony, ready to draw their weapons despite the overwhelming numbers arrayed before them.

Sir Richard remained seated on his great warhorse as he gazed down at the Greek. "We seek entrance to –"

The foreman drew his sword slowly and, methodically, moved into a defensive stance. "You've already been down there," he growled, his dark eyes blazing. "You came back too, and killed innocent men!"

Sir Richard returned his stare steadily for a moment before he lifted his left leg up and over and slipped off the back of his mount onto the ground.

"We are going down again," he moved forward until his face was almost touching the foreman's. "Whether you like it or not. So get your lackeys out

61

of the way. Now!"

The Greek's head spun and he nodded at his men who instantly drew their swords and stood ready to defend the tunnel entrance.

"You are *not* going down again! That is consecrated ground – holy ground. We know you defiled it last night. We know you started a fire in our village last night. We know" – he pushed his face up against the Hospitaller knight's – "it was you who butchered our friends."

By now, Jacob had dismounted as well and stood behind his master's right shoulder defensively, his sword held by his side as another English voice rang out from the darkness behind them.

"Are you deaf? We *are* going down there, and you aren't going to stop us! Now...move the fuck aside before we tear the lot of you apart!"

Sir Richard shot a surprised glance to his left and saw the bluff Yorkshireman, Stephen, still mounted on his great warhorse and pointing his longsword at the foreman. The Greek was visibly taken aback by the force of the sergeant's admonition, so Richard made the most of the opportunity, reaching out his gauntleted hand to grasp the man around the neck in a vice-like grip.

"You fucking heard the sergeant!" he roared, his voice deafening in the charged atmosphere. "Move your arses out of our way or we'll move them for you!"

Outnumbered more than six-to-one as they were, Sir Richard expected the guards to back down. Instead, he found his blade instinctively swinging up across his body as one of the tunnel guards tried to cut him in half.

As the steel met with a dull metallic clang the Hospitaller roared in anger. "Attack!" He batted his opponent's blade to the side, hammered his left, gauntleted fist into the man's face then stabbed him in the stomach.

The Greek guards appeared to have no fear of death though, throwing themselves recklessly at the Hospitallers, swords flailing wildly with cries of hatred bursting forth from their lips.

Jacob ducked as a sword whistled past his ear, rising to slam his right shoulder into his attacker's chest, throwing the man stumbling backwards. The sergeant pulled his arm back and rammed the point of his sword into his attacker's midriff.

The man fell to the ground, blood trickling from the side of his mouth, black eyes staring up at Jacob while making a strangely disturbing groaning sound that seemed to come from deep in his chest.

On his other side, the dour Yorkshireman, Stephen, traded blows back and forth with another of the Greek guards, the sounds of steel on steel reverberating deafeningly in the arid night atmosphere before the guard slipped, falling to one knee with his sword hand outstretched to break his fall.

Stephen's longsword swept mercilessly down, hammering into the guard's neck with horrific force, the jolt shuddering along the Hospitaller's arm as his victim's neck was shorn through and the head toppled to the ground in a hideous gout of blood, only a long, thin flap of skin keeping it attached to the body.

In the space of a few moments the guards'

numbers had been whittled down by more than half, but the remainder came on despite that, screaming in fury, their black eyes cold and apparently fearless.

Sir Jean de Pagnac stabbed his blade into one attacker's thigh, while Sir Richard turned and batted the final guard's weapon aside and leaned in to smash his forehead against the man's face. As he fell, blood already beginning to stream down his face and around his thick lips, the Hospitaller leaned forward and slid the point of his sword into the man's neck, opening a huge wound that carried his life away in a wave of crimson.

In the calm that followed the shocking violence all that could be heard was the sound of laboured breathing as the victorious Hospitallers sucked in air, trying to regain their equilibrium.

The fight had been an easy one. Not one of the Hospitallers had so much as a scratch on them – indeed most of them hadn't even had to strike a blow. And yet...

The ferocity and single-minded fury of the tunnel's unskilled defenders had shaken the soldiers who still had to make their way down the staircase in the sands and enter the foreboding tunnel.

Whatever drove these devil-worshippers was enough to impel them to fight to the death even against insurmountable odds.

"That was...strange," Sir Jean said, looking at his knightly counterpart. "Badly outnumbered, and by this lot," he waved a gauntleted hand back at the impressive-looking force behind him. "Yet those men chose to give their lives in defence of this shrine or whatever it is."

"They fought like they were possessed," Stephen agreed, looking around at the shadowy village. "This place has an evil, twisted feeling."

Sir Richard wiped the blood from his blade on a dead guard's gambeson before sheathing the weapon and turning to face the rest of the men. "Indeed," he looked at Sir Jean and Stephen. "Whatever's going on down here has pervaded the entire village. If we don't do something about it now, it could spread throughout the whole island and our Order will find itself homeless again." He patted Jacob on the shoulder and addressed Sir Jean. "My sergeant and I have been told of another entrance to this tainted shrine, where hopefully we'll come face-to-face with the leaders of this religion. We'll head there now, while you take the rest of the men down into the tunnel and make sure no-one escapes when I interrupt whatever blasphemous rite they're in the middle of."

"Assuming that informant's information was right," Jacob muttered.

"Leontios has led us right so far," Sir Richard retorted. "I believe his story, now...let's move."

Sir Jean de Pagnac nodded as his superior officer rode into the darkness with his faithful sergeant-at-arms, then ordered two of the mercenaries to guard the rest of their horses.

At the bottom of the staircase Stephen lifted the latch on the great door into the shrine and slipped inside, the remaining Hospitallers following at his back.

* * *

65

Krymmeni Thesi's church was a small building, but sturdily built from the local sandstone and appeared well maintained. There was a large three-barred crucifix above the small but functional altar and crude but pleasant enough paintings showed scenes from Christ's life, death and rebirth.

It seemed to be nothing more than a normal Orthodox church. There was nothing openly sacrilegious about the place. No obscene bas-reliefs had been carved into the walls and the book that lay open on the marble altar was just a bible.

As they tied their mounts to a post outside Sir Richard held up an armoured hand and the two soldiers stopped in their tracks, breath held, senses straining.

The sound of men speaking could be heard, muffled by the heavy stone and oak construction of the building, but it appeared to come from the vestry, to the rear of the altar through a narrow doorway.

The knight drew his dagger, knowing a sword would be nothing more than a hindrance within the cramped confines of the church and Jacob followed his lead as they crept through the doorway, the muted voices becoming louder as they went.

"Leave one alive," Sir Richard whispered.

They walked silently into the vestry where two Greeks stood chatting. They had short wooden sticks by their sides and looked dangerous, each of them being a fair bit taller and broader than either of the Hospitallers.

"Hey!"

The men spun at the unexpected voice, hands

reaching out instinctively for their weapons, large dark eyes wide at the intrusion.

The nearest of them roared in anger and charged, his massive bulk bearing down on Jacob, ready to slam the smaller Englishman into the wall.

Before he could reach the sergeant Sir Richard threw himself shoulder first into the charging Greek, slowing his momentum and sending him barrelling sideways into the wall. At the same time the knight punched his dagger deep into the man's groin, feeling warm blood spill onto his hand despite the gauntlet he wore. He pulled the blade free and the man landed with a gasp on his backside, the breath blown from his lungs and his life-force oozing from the mortal wound.

The second of the men stood stock-still, eyeing the Hospitallers warily, but with no fear in his black eyes, only anger.

"What do you men want?" he demanded.

"We need to know how to get into the underground cavern," Sir Richard replied as he moved forward, Jacob following a little way to the left, giving their opponent two oncoming targets to worry about.

The man's gaze flicked between his silently approaching opponents, sweat beading on his finely wrinkled brow. "I wouldn't tell you Catholic scum where it is," he spat. "Even if I knew."

Beneath the ground, the rhythmic sound of a chant could faintly be heard and Sir Richard knew they had to act fast before any more innocents like the earlier night's couple were sacrificed.

"Get him," he grunted, launching himself at the

man who tried desperately to defend himself, swinging his wooden cudgel around and grinning as he felt it connect with the knight's bicep.

The cultist's pleasure was short-lived though, as Jacob moved in and hammered his chain-mailed elbow into the man's mouth, smashing teeth and bone.

Reeling but still alert, the guard's cudgel came round again, but Jacob threw his arm up, deflecting the blow harmlessly to the side and again battered his elbow into the cultist's face.

This time the man stumbled and fell, landing shakily on one knee, and the sergeant-at-arms punched him in the side of the head, knocking him to the ground where he lay, cursing under his breath but too groggy to rise and defend himself.

"How do we get down there?" Sir Richard demanded, grasping the man by the hair and yanking his head up viciously.

"Fuck you!"

The Hospitaller slammed the pommel of his dagger into the cultist's cheek, drawing a howl of agony from the man whose sinister black-pupiled glare turned at last from defiant to frightened. He tried to mask his anxiety by spitting in his inquisitor's face, but didn't have the strength and the bloody glob ran down his chin pitifully.

"Listen to me," Sir Richard said. "You can get out of this alive if you tell us how to get into the cavern from here. We're going to torture you until you do. So tell us now and save yourself a lot of pain."

The man thought about it for a moment, emotions creasing his sun-darkened face as he struggled to decide what to do before, almost hysterically, he screamed another "Fuck you!" at the Hospitallers.

The chanting from underground had grown louder. They didn't have time for this.

"Tell us, now!" Jacob roared, stamping down on the cultist's calf. The crack of bone snapping echoed around the room and the man screamed in rage.

"Tell us!" Sir Richard repeated his sergeant's order, but the whimpering man simply shook his head.

Jacob leaned down, dagger in hand and pressed the tip against the man's rectum. "You *will* tell us, right fucking *now,* how to get into that cavern or I'll stick this up your filthy arse." He pressed on the blade, the point piercing the man's clothing and drawing blood.

It was enough.

The heretic, tears of humiliation coursing down his cheeks, told them what they wanted to know before Sir Richard knocked him out cold with another blow to the side of the head.

"We're leaving him alive?" Jacob asked incredulously as his master tied the man's hands behind his back and left him face down on the hard stone floor.

"Aye," Sir Richard replied. "He told us what we wanted to know, didn't he? He's no threat now so I'm not murdering him while he lies there unconscious, there's no honour in that. Come on, let's get into that cavern!"

* * *

The chanting had grown louder as Stephen and Sir Jean de Pagnac led the Hospitaller force along the gloomy corridor to the cavern. Whatever ceremony the blasphemers were performing tonight was well under-way, judging from the near-hysterical shouting that assailed them as they neared the great chamber.

"Our job is to stop anyone from escaping," Sir Jean reminded the men behind him. "Don't kill anyone unless they're a threat. Hopefully these blasphemers will come along without a fuss."

Stephen laughed, cocking an ear in the direction of the chanting. "Are you hearing what I'm hearing?" he asked his master. "You think that lot are going to come along quietly, without a fight?"

Sir Jean spread his hands wide, the torchlight flickering off his immaculate blade. "We can but hope," he replied. "My sergeant is right, though," he said, louder, turning so the mercenaries behind him would all be able to hear his words. "It's more than likely these people will defend this insane god they worship with their lives. So be it. If they attack us, kill them without compunction. If we can take prisoners, though, so much the better. A show trial and public executions will deter others from following this filthy 'god' of theirs."

As they neared the cavern they saw more guards arrayed before them. The devil-worshippers had learned their lesson from Sir Richard and Jacob's previous visit and had placed half-a-dozen armed men at the end of the tunnel to stop any more intruders. They hadn't expected a force as large as this, obviously, or there would have been more of them, but even so, Sir Jean knew after their earlier fight with the guards at the front door that these men would not back down, even in the face of their imminent doom.

"Take them!" Sir Jean ordered, pointing his sword at the guardsmen, who all had the same sinister black-pupilled eyes as well as bucklers and short-swords. One of them detached himself from the main party and sprinted down the nearest flight of stairs, no doubt to raise the alarm. "Take them!" the knight repeated.

The men behind him, Stephen included, streamed around him, swords drawn, and engaged the blasphemers efficiently and ruthlessly.

Although the men under Sir Jean's command weren't brother-knights, or even sergeants for the most part, they did wear decent quality light armour, carried sharpened blades of high-quality steel and had been given good training. The guards on the other hand were simple villagers. Poorly armed and untrained they fought with the fury and single-minded belief of religious fanatics, but they were too unskilled to stand against the Hospitallers and the one-sided battle was over within moments.

Sir Jean moved past the bodies to look down on the still chanting congregation below. The guard that had run to raise the alarm was waving his arms towards the altar but the shouts of "Arra! Arra! Arra! Dagon! Dagon! Dagon!" filled the air as the masked priest bent to cut the throat of a woman who struggled against the burly worshippers holding her down against the cold stone until her life-force drained from her body and she lay still.

The priest obviously couldn't hear the guard's warning, and the congregation were too far gone in their murderous ecstasy to take any notice of yet another excited man shouting at them.

Stephen stared at the horrific tableau beneath, his eyes flaring in outrage at the sight of the dead woman and the two children that stood, screaming in grief and terror behind her lifeless corpse. He turned to look at his master, Sir Jean de Pagnac. "In God's name, we can take no prisoners here," he growled. "These bastards deserve no mercy."

The French knight nodded. "I agree. We should wait until Sir Richard appears though. If we just start wading into them the priest might escape out the back door in the confusion and take his twisted religion to some other village."

"Well Sir Richard better hurry up then," the sergeant-at-arms replied, turning back to the hideous ritual below. "It looks like the priest has a young woman to sacrifice after the two children."

* * *

As they hurried through the dark tunnel underneath St Luke's – a cramped, low affair this one, which looked like it might collapse upon them at any moment – Sir Richard and his cursing sergeant-at-arms could hear the euphoric shouts of the gathered worshippers and knew it signalled the end of some other poor bastard's

72

life in the name of this ancient Dagon.

"Come on!" Sir Richard raised his pace as the chanting, rather than falling away after the sacrifice, continued at the same volume. "They must have another victim lined up!"

Their cautious jog became a breathless sprint, the desire to prevent the death of yet another innocent proving greater than their own sense of personal safety.

The tunnel was short, praise God, and they barrelled into the great cavern, blades held before them defensively as their eyes adjusted to the light and their ears rang from the chants of the gathered throng.

"Arra! Arra! Dagon!"

The masked high-priest stood at the sacrificial altar which had by now been cleared of its previous incumbent, ready for the two sobbing children that were held by the two burly heretics behind the altar.

"They've got the children from St Luke's," Sir Richard muttered, watching in horror as the corpse of the woman whose husband had been taken in his sleep by Dagon was dragged over to the grimy stonework that channelled the sacrificial victims' blood below and dumped into it like a sack of rubbish.

"Stop them!" Sir Richard screamed, legs pumping as he tried to cover the distance to the stone altar, Jacob following in his wake. "In the name of Christ, stop them!"

The children were lifted onto the great stone altar and held down by the worshippers before the priest moved from one to the other with his wicked sacrificial knife. Their high-pitched cries trailed off, blood streaming onto the stone below and the priest calmly walked over to stand behind the young woman who watched as the terrible rite was carried out.

"Athenais!" Jacob cried, taking in the scene before them in shock. "They're going to sacrifice Athenais next!"

The priest turned as he heard the girl's name shouted, tearing the mask from his face to stare, glassy-eyed and confused at the intruders who were running furiously towards him.

"Christ above.." Sir Richard's sword dropped as he realised who it was. Father Vitus. Leontios had been right!

"You little bastard!"

Jacob roared in fury at the sight of the murderous priest standing before the pretty girl he'd grown fond of and lunged at the Greek who had brought them into this whole thing in the first place. Father Vitus never even attempted to move as the point of the Hospitaller sergeant's longsword hammered into his chest and tore through his back in a shower of blood.

The chanting had slowed and finally, now, stopped, as the bemused congregation looked on, unsure what was happening.

The priest's legs slowly gave way and the dead weight was too much for Jacob to hold. He pulled the blade free with a damp sucking sound that seemed to reverberate around the cyclopean cavern.

Sir Richard looked up towards the balcony above and found Sir Jean. "Take them into custody!" he roared into the silence. "Kill any who resist!" He stood, numb, looking down at the children who, just a few nights earlier, had cried out to him in St Luke's when their father had been taken in his sleep and tears spilled from his eyes. How could he let this happen to them? An image of his own young sons – Simon and Edward – filled his mind and he began to sob with the horror of it all.

In the cavern around him Dagon's followers finally realised they were under attack but, without an effective leader, simply looked about themselves wondering what they should do.

"Athenais!" Jacob sheathed his sword, still covered in Father Vitus's warm blood, and moved towards the priest's housekeeper, his arms open, a reassuring smile on his open face. "You're safe now, Athenais. Our men are coming down those stairs to take these bastard devil-worshippers away for trial. You're safe now."

The young woman looked down at Vitus's corpse before turning her dark eyes back to Jacob.

"That's more than can be said for you, fool," she growled, producing the same sacrificial knife Vitus had used earlier from behind her back and shoving it into the sergeant's throat.

Blood erupted from the wound and Sir Richard looked on in shock, surprised that his sergeant's head didn't fall from his shoulders, the cut was so vicious.

As Jacob fell to his knees Athenais kicked him into the gutter that collected the blood from the their victims, nodding in satisfaction as the thick crimson fluid pumped from the Hospitaller's wound, filling the gutter. "Vitus was nothing more than my puppet," she laughed. "He was smitten by my occasional sexual favours and the belladonna – amongst other things – that I secretly tipped into his wine to keep him pliable."

Dagon's High Priestess looked up into Sir Richard's tear-stained face, the bloody dagger held in front of her savage grin. "Now it's your turn to meet Dagon, Sir Knight. Come to me!"

* * *

Behind Athenais the congregation had really begun to panic. Not only was a force of Hospitallers coming at them, swords drawn, but the thumping noises they'd been hearing for weeks deep under their village had begun again only now they were much, much louder. The cavern shook with the thunderous rumbling as Sir Richard faced Father Vitus's supposed housekeeper.

"He is coming," she laughed. Her face looked innocent and pretty and she smiled like a child enjoying a game. It just added to the horror Sir Richard felt at what was happening around him.

"Arra! Arra! Arra! Dagon! Dagon! Dagon!"

Some of the congregation joined in with her chant but by now the Hospitallers had reached the bottom of the stairs and were moving in amongst them.

"Kill them," Athenais screamed, her face seeming to glow with joy. "Kill every one of them! Dagon will be here soon to reward your sacrifice!"

The congregation threw themselves at the Hospitallers, hammering their fists, knees, teeth and whatever else they had against their heavily armoured opponents.

Sir Jean de Pagnac looked on from halfway down the stairs, his eyes wide in disbelief. "Take no prisoners!" he roared, making his way down to do his part. "Wipe these blasphemers from God's Earth."

Athenais grinned even wider, black eyes betraying her joy at the Hospitaller knight's command. "That's it, spill their blood; let it run like water into the pool!"

Sir Richard made to attack her but four of the screaming heretics came for him – empty-handed but with an insane, murderous gleam in their eyes – as she walked forward to stand gazing down into a great hole in the stone floor.

"He is coming!" Athenais screamed, her voice surprisingly powerful, filling the entire cavern and everyone, cultist and Hospitaller alike, stopped as they recognized the portent in her words. "He is coming..."

Something arose from the black opening in the floor. It appeared to be nothing more than smoke at first, but Sir Richard felt the hairs on the back of his neck rise as the terrible outline started to take shape revealing the same hideously long limbs and blank, faceless head that had haunted his dreams. He looked around at his men and wondered if he was hallucinating as none of the other Hospitallers seemed to notice the amorphous shape, all eyes except his own still fixed on the smiling High-Priestess.

"Stand down!" Sir Richard roared, his powerful voice loud enough, just, to reach the men he commanded here. "Stand down! The blood we're spilling is bringing that monstrosity to life!" It was obvious to him that the villagers weren't all here voluntarily – some of them didn't bear the black pupils of the faithful, and many were trying to escape from the cavern now as the knights closed in. But some of the villagers – even if they didn't follow Dagon – hated the Catholic Hospitallers and appeared happy to rise against these knights who'd taken over their island and repressed their own Orthodox Christianity.

Athenais lunged at Sir Richard as he contemplated all this, throwing him back, and he struggled to maintain his footing.

"Your men might butcher my followers," she shouted over the cacophony that filled the air as the men and women behind her fell to the Hospitallers' blades. "But their lifeblood will resurrect Dagon." She turned again to her people who, by now, were lost in blood-lust as they sought to defend themselves against the Hospitallers. "Throw yourselves on their swords!" she screamed, grinning maniacally at Sir Richard. "Dagon will resurrect you when he takes form again."

It was impossible for the Hospitallers to stop fighting the villagers without committing suicide. The people came at them, bare-handed but with savage, murderous intent, and the red surcoats of the soldiers became slick with the blood of the crazed – or simply terrified – worshippers.

On the altar lay the book Father Vitus had been reading from in what sounded like Arabic to Sir Richard. As Athenais lunged at him again he side-stepped her blow and punched her in the jaw, sending her sprawling on the ground where she lay, groaning, her sacrificial dagger spinning away to the side.

The knight ran past her and grabbed the book, which felt strangely clammy in his hands and seemed to move as if it were alive. He barely noticed the title on the spine –*Necronomicon* – as he lifted it and hurled it into the pit.

He'd hoped removing the cursed book would somehow halt the smoky figure's return to corporeal form but it didn't. Dagon, or whatever the thing was, continued to become more substantial and Sir Richard felt the icy grasp of fear grip him.

"Stephen!" Sir Jean's sergeant-at-arms had fought his way to the front of the altar and he turned to face Sir Richard now.

"Sir Jean's done for!" the sergeant cried over the sound of dying. "Went down under half-a-dozen of these lunatics."

"You have to get out of here," Sir Richard replied. "Take word to the Grand Master. I don't know what he can do to stop...that...But...he has to return with more men and destroy this whole place! Go – the rest of us'll do our best to hold the bastards off!"

"Look out!"

Stephen's warning cry came just in time. Sir Richard turned and saw just a glimpse of movement coming towards his head. He dodged backwards as Athenais swung a heavy candlestick at him, catching him a glancing blow on the temple, but her momentum carried her forward. As the Hospitaller knight lost consciousness the last thing he saw was the girl, screaming in terror as she fell into the pit with her murderous god.

* * *

"Are you seriously – seriously! – telling me some demon wiped out your entire force? Including a knight? You two and a couple of mercenaries are the only survivors?" Foulques de Villaret looked more bemused than angry, despite his raised voice.

Sir Richard bowed his head in acknowledgement of his disastrous mission and his superior's scathing words. "What I've told you is the truth. Whether we are the only survivors we have no way of knowing without going back to Krymmeni Thesi and searching the cavern. Please," he looked up at his superior, his voice earnest, "let us lead a force back there, today – now! – to rescue any of our brothers that remain alive, and to avenge Jacob's murder."

De Villaret stared thoughtfully at the two Englishmen before him, wondering if they'd lost their minds or if their ridiculous tale could possibly be real.

"I thought you didn't believe in all this supernatural nonsense, Richard...?"

The bearded knight looked away uncomfortably before replying. "Before all this happened, if I'd heard the tale from someone else I'd have thought them touched but now..." He met his superior's gaze earnestly. "I have to believe the evidence of my own eyes, Grand Master."

"You – sergeant!" Stephen snapped to attention as the Grand Master turned his glare on him. "You agree with this story? You saw this demon too?"

The Yorkshireman shook his head slightly, almost apologetically, as if he was betraying the big knight at his side. "No, Grand Master, I didn't see the demon myself, I must admit… But I can vouch for Sir Richard's story; everything else happened as he described."

"Very well," de Villaret growled after a time. "We'll go to the village and see what's left of our men. But you're not leading this time Richard. I'm coming with you; I want to see for myself what in God's name this is all about."

A short time later, two hundred Hospitallers, many of them high-ranking knights or sergeants rather than just the mercenaries of the previous mission, rode out of the fortress and headed for the accursed village that had caused their Order so much trouble.

When Sir Richard had passed out in the cavern Stephen had carried him back through the same cramped tunnel the knight had come along with Jacob. It had been a hellish flight as he struggled not to hit Sir Richard's head or legs off the walls, the sounds of fighting slowly dying away as the heretics were killed. As he made it to the way out and breathlessly climbed the stairs that would take him into the church above the distant sounds changed. The screams became ones of terror and despair rather than the ecstatic cries of the crazed, dying worshippers. Horrific thunderous noises filled the air, echoing along the tunnel and causing the ground to shake as if an earthquake was upon them.

Gasping a prayer of thanks to God, Stephen at

last made it back to the church, his burden causing his arms to burn as he hurried past the incongruously normal looking pews and out into the night. Sobbing in desperation he struggled to haul the unconscious knight onto the big destrier that stood tied up by the door, its nostrils flaring fearfully at the sounds and tremors from underground.

He had freed the second beast then pulled himself up behind Sir Richard and kicked his heels into their mount which was only too happy to race out of Krymmeni Thesi and back to the fortress despite its burden. As he'd passed the tunnel entrance Stephen had screamed at the two young mercenaries who'd been left to guard the horses there to follow him back to the citadel.

"Is that horse of yours all right?" de Villaret asked, watching Sir Richard's mount as they approached the village again now. "Looks a bit nervous."

"He'll be fine, Grand Master," the knight replied, patting the destrier's neck comfortingly. "He's been in battles before."

"Not with a demon, he hasn't," Stephen muttered under his breath. The English sergeant-at-arms, his own master murdered by the devil-worshippers, had taken up position beside Sir Richard since Jacob was also lying dead beneath Krymmeni Thesi.

The Grand Master made a dismissive sound, but his eyes turned to look into the field they were passing. "What the hell's that man doing?"

"It's a straw man," Sir Richard replied without looking over.

De Villaret shrugged and the enormous force of armoured men rode into the village as the sun sat high in the sky overhead, making the air almost unbearably hot for those amongst the Knights that had grown up in colder climes.

Krymmeni Thesi bustled; all appeared normal. Just a village like any other on the island. The women and children gazed up fearfully at the mounted soldiers while the men at work in the streets looked at them warily as they passed by, heading for the church.

"I have to say," de Villaret said. "This place doesn't look like a demon was brought to life here only a few hours ago."

They reached the church and dismounted. Sir Richard didn't answer the Grand Master and neither did Stephen; both men were apprehensive at going back into the cavern to find...what?

"Well there's no way we can get all these men down here at once," de Villaret noted as the big English knight took him beneath the church to the tunnel entrance. "But I hear no sounds of fighting, or screams of dying men, or growls from devils. I believe we'll be safe enough without an escort. You and the sergeant wait here while we" – he gestured to five other high-ranking knights to follow – "search this cavern of yours."

"Arrogant prick," Stephen grumbled as the Hospitaller's leader entered the tunnel with supreme confidence.

Sir Richard gave a nervous smile in reply. The Grand Master *was* an arrogant bastard he thought – one of these days it would come back to haunt him.

A short time later the sound of men running came to them and Sir Richard drew his sword, licking his lips as he stared at the doorway. "Swords at the ready, men," he ordered, feeling no safer despite the presence of so many hard fighting men right behind him.

Foulques de Villaret appeared, his chosen knights close on his heels, every one of the small party with faces pale and eyes wide in shock.

"Close it up!" the Grand Master shouted, nervously glancing back over his shoulder apparently for signs of pursuit. "Close this entrance up, now, so no one else will ever be able to use it! Block the tunnel with stones, rubble, those pews – *anything* you can find! Then seal the entrance with cement and burn this place to the ground along with everything in it. We'll remove the stone it's built with over time. I want nothing left of this accursed place!"

"Sir? What did you see? Did the blasphemers kill all our men?"

"Stop wasting time and follow my orders!" the Grand Master snapped back at Sir Richard. "All the men are dead, yes, although I don't think any human could have done...*that* to their bodies..."

He and his small retinue stumbled out onto the street, some of them retching, and Sir Richard looked over at Stephen and the rest of the men. "You heard him, get to work!"

The Hospitallers spent the rest of the morning blocking the tunnel before they set alight to the church, watching as the wooden roof collapsed upon itself. Then they moved on to the other entrance, the one Sir Richard and Jacob had first discovered and sealed that off with rubble and cement too.

When they were done the prior performed a mass for the souls of their fallen brothers, buried beneath the village for the rest of time.

The ceremony ended and Foulques de Villaret beckoned Sir Richard over to him as the sun began to sink in the sky, the relentless, hellish heat giving way to a refreshing easterly breeze.

"The devil-worshippers," he said, "you reported that they have black eyes, am I right? Their pupils are so wide they cover almost the entire eyeball?"

The Englishman nodded, thinking back over the recent days' events. "Aye, Grand Master, all of them had that queer look about them."

De Villaret nodded. "Good. You and the sergeant may return to the fortress; your investigation is finished."

"Grand Master? Are you not coming with us? What about the men? What arc we going to do about Dagon?"

"The men will stay with me. We have more work to do here."

"Work? What do" –

"You've already seen enough, Sir Richard," de Villaret broke in. "What happened in that cavern cannot be blamed on you. So I'm sparing you any further mental anguish. Return to the city. When I come back we will look at finding a new posting for you, perhaps back in your homeland."

The English knight inclined his head, cursing inwardly, and moved towards his horse, calling for Stephen to follow him.

As the two Englishmen rode from the village Grand Master Foulques de Villaret gave orders to his knights. The Hospitallers then moved from house to house, searching them for anyone who carried the strange eyes Sir Richard had described.

Not many were found; no more than twenty or so. De Villaret surmised most of them had been cut down during the previous night's perverted underground ceremony.

"Bind them," he told the knights. "And bring them with us."

The villagers cried out for mercy. The black-eyed people that had been arrested were their husbands, wives, mothers, fathers, children....

The thought of these families being infested by the unholy sect terrified de Villaret who had seen the fearsome power of this blasphemous religion in the cavern beneath the sand he stood on now.

This cult had to be destroyed without mercy.

"Move out!" he roared, mounting his enormous warhorse. "If any of these people try to stop you, cut them down!"

The column slowly wound its way back towards the city, leaving behind the wailing villagers whom de Villaret ordered be stopped from following them.

When they reached the field with the sinister straw man in it the Grand Master called a halt, grunting to himself as he noticed the straw effigy was no longer standing there. A chill ran down his neck,

86

and he raised his voice, desperate for this whole thing to be done with.

"Take these people into the field and behead them," he ordered. "Then burn the bodies."

Sir Raymond de Balben nodded. He too had been in the cavern. "What about the children?"

"Them too."

* * *

The ship creaked and groaned as it picked up speed and left Rhodes behind on its long journey back to England. Stephen felt sick already and even Sir Richard felt apprehensive at the unfamiliar sounds and sensations sea travel brought.

Grand Master de Villaret had, after talking to his Turcopolier Thomas L'Archer – a friend of Sir Richard's – decided to give the English knight command of the preceptory at Kirklees in Yorkshire, where he had family ties; indeed, his wife and two young sons were living with family there right now and the knight was looking forward tremendously to seeing them all again.

De Villaret also assigned Stephen to replace Jacob as the English knight's new sergeant-at-arms.

The pair stood now in the glorious sunshine, leaning on the ship's railing and gazing back across the sparkling blue waves at Rhodes as the ship rolled on the gentle waves, the ruins of the Colossus still dominating the scene even though most of the great monument had been destroyed by an earthquake generations ago.

"You glad to be leaving the island?" Stephen asked, more to take his mind off the nausea he felt at the rocking motion of the ship than from any desire to make small-talk.

Sir Richard nodded firmly. "Aye, I am. I'd have liked to carry on the investigation but the Grand Master wants to erase the whole thing from history. He's ordered the entire population of Krymmeni Thesi to be dispersed around other settlements so he can wipe the place from the face of the Earth. I'm happy to leave Rhodes for now and go back to my family – you heard what that villager from Kailithies reported this morning."

As they'd made ready to depart from the fortress earlier that day a man had arrived from Kailithies, a small village not far from Krymmeni Thesi, to seek an audience with the Grand Master. He claimed strange sounds had recently been heard from beneath the countryside surrounding the village – loud thumps and unintelligible, blasphemous voices chanting.

Sir Richard, hearing the news from another knight, had suggested to de Villaret that he hire the merchant, Leontios, to inscribe more of the flat stones with the mysterious symbols on them and secrete them all over the island in the hope they'd offer some protection against Dagon. The Grand Master hadn't been enthusiastic about the idea of employing an Orthodox Greek to plant heathen symbology on his island but in light of the worrying news from Kailithies had relented.

After Sir Richard had located the Greek merchant and enlisted his aid for the Order – with a further payment of silver coins for his previous help – they'd bade each other a respectful farewell and the knight led his new sergeant to the docks where their ship back to the north of England awaited them.

They stood on the deck in silence for a time now, drinking in the sight of the slowly receding island in the sun, the occasional spot of greenery standing out beautifully against the sandstone of the port and the clear blue of the ocean, lost in their memories of what had happened in Krymmeni Thesi.

"What d'you think happened to that...devil you saw?" Stephen wondered. "Did our mercenaries stop it before it could take physical form? Did they kill it?"

The Hospitaller knight had asked himself the same question repeatedly but would never be sure. "Who knows?" he replied. "Dagon, or whatever that thing was, wasn't alive to begin with; it was just smoke drifting in the air. You can't kill something that's already dead. Maybe it was just a figment of my imagination. No one else saw it, did they?" He crossed himself with a shake of his head and reached inside his surcoat to grip the flat stone with the elder sign inscribed on it that Leontios had given him.

Rhodes was left further and further behind as the wind filled their sails and the horrors they'd witnessed there seemed to diminish into the horizon along with the island itself.

"Aye, I'll be glad to get a fresh start back in England," Sir Richard said with a small smile, beginning to relax for the first time in what seemed like weeks. "It'll be an easy life for us I'm sure. England's mostly at peace and Kirklees is a comfortable estate. We won't need to worry too much about ancient demons there. The only thing we'll need to be wary of are the outlaws – I hear Barnsdale's full of them..."

AUTHOR'S NOTE

Readers of my two full-length novels, *Wolf's Head* and *The Wolf and the Raven* will know some of Sir Richard and Stephen's story already, but ever since I was writing *Raven* I thought they were such good characters that it'd be interesting to look into their background in a little more depth, hence this novella which is, I suppose, something of a prequel to *Wolf's Head*.

I've tried to write my previous novels from a "realistic" standpoint, so for this work I decided it'd be fun to introduce some minor fantasy or supernatural elements. Dagon comes from an HP Lovecraft story (and is also an ancient Sumerian god) although the "Arra! Dagon!" chant comes from a song by the brilliant death metal band Nile (thank you Karl, Dallas and George!) and my description of him here is based on the recent internet invention Slenderman. The black-eyed people are also taken from modern, internet folklore – search for "black-eyed kids" for some spooky stories...!

I would have liked to include some of the folklore indigenous to Rhodes but was unable to find anything other than cats and sleep-paralysis. The latter is something I suffer from periodically and trust me, it really is as terrifying as I've depicted it here the first few times it happens. Even now, after years of dealing with it, I find it frightening when it happens. I've never seen Dagon but I did see an archetypal 'grey' alien walk into my bedroom and stand beside

91

my bed staring at me when I was about 20. It was a genuinely frightening experience although I didn't wake up with a sore arse so I'm hoping I wasn't *really* abducted into a UFO...

Grand Master Foulques de Villaret was a real person, and he was a rather arrogant individual – a group of his own Hospitaller Knights attempted to assassinate him in 1317 because of his tyrannical behaviour, so I tried to bring some of that out in the story.

I really hope you enjoyed *Knight of the Cross*, whether you're a new reader or someone who's read my previous work. If you did, please leave a review on Amazon, Goodreads and wherever else you like to talk about books, it really does help a self-published author like myself – I don't have an agent to tell people about my work, so I'm reliant on my readers and I greatly appreciate the feedback.

My next novel will be the third in The Forest Lord series and takes up where *The Wolf and the Raven* left off, so keep an eye out for it. The working title is *Rise of the Wolf* and it should be out around the end of 2014/ early 2015. In the meantime, I'm working on an audio version of *Knight of the Cross* with Nick Ellsworth who brilliantly read the *Wolf's Head* audiobook so look out for that (it should be cheap, as it's a lot shorter than a full-length novel, so if you ever wanted to try an audiobook, now's the time...).

Thanks to Robin Carter for his insightful editing suggestions, to Romina Nicolaides for her invaluable insights into Greek culture, and thank YOU for buying *Knight of the Cross*!

Steven A. McKay,
Old Kilpatrick,
August 8th, 2014

Keep up to date with my writing and join in with the discussions and give-aways here:

www.Facebook.com/RobinHoodNovel

http://stevenamckay.wordpress.com

Made in the USA
Charleston, SC
20 September 2014